SECRETS and LEGENDS

VICTORY LANE
by Marisa Carroll

From the opening green flag at Daytona to the final checkered flag at Homestead, the competition will be fierce for the NASCAR Sprint Cup Series championship.

The **Grosso** family practically has engine oil in their veins. For them racing represents not just a way of life but a tradition that goes back to NASCAR's inception. Like all families, they also have a few skeletons to hide. What happens when someone peeks inside the closet becomes a matter that threatens to destroy them.

The **Murphys** have been supporting drivers in the pits for generations, despite a vendetta with the Grossos that's almost as old as NASCAR itself! But the Murphys have their own secrets... and a few indiscretions that could cost them everything.

The **Branches** are newcomers, and some would say upstarts. But as this affluent Texas family is further enmeshed in the world of NASCAR, they become just as embroiled in the intrigues on and off the track.

The **Motor Media Group** are the PR people responsible for the positive public perception of NASCAR's stars. They are the glue that repairs the damage. And more than anything, they feel the brunt of the backlash....

These NASCAR families have secrets to hide, and reputations to protect. This season will test them all.

Dear Reader,

Victory Lane is our second contribution to the series NASCAR: SECRETS AND LEGENDS. We loved writing this book because it allowed us to take another look at the intertwined lives of the Grosso and Murphy families.

We're thrilled to be able to tell Dean and Patsy Grosso's story. Their thirty-year marriage is on the rocks—it looks as if Dean will have to choose between his last chance at a championship season and the woman he loves. And while we learn in this book, who was responsible for the deaths of Troy and Connor Murphy, we also discover that these two legendary NASCAR families have other momentous secrets they've yet to share.

Please join us in the conclusion of NASCAR: SECRETS AND LEGENDS, and follow us back into the exciting world of NASCAR in 2009 with *No Holds Barred* and *Into the Corner*, available next year in Harlequin's officially licensed NASCAR romance series.

Till later,

Carol Wagner and Marian Franz
(Marisa Carroll)

NASCAR

VICTORY LANE

Marisa Carroll

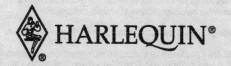

HARLEQUIN®

TORONTO • NEW YORK • LONDON
AMSTERDAM • PARIS • SYDNEY • HAMBURG
STOCKHOLM • ATHENS • TOKYO • MILAN • MADRID
PRAGUE • WARSAW • BUDAPEST • AUCKLAND

Recycling programs
for this product may
not exist in your area.

ISBN-13: 978-0-373-21799-1
ISBN-10:   0-373-21799-4

VICTORY LANE

Copyright © 2008 by Harlequin Books S.A.

Carol I. Wagner and Marian L. Franz are acknowledged
as the authors of this work.

NASCAR® and the NASCAR Library Collection® are registered trade-
marks of the National Association for Stock Car Auto Racing, Inc.

This edition published by arrangement with Harlequin Books S.A.

www.eHarlequin.com

Printed in U.S.A.

MARISA CARROLL

is the pen name of authors Carol Wagner and Marian Franz. The team has been writing bestselling books for almost twenty-five years. During that time they have published more than forty-five titles, most for the Harlequin Superromance line, and are the recipients of several industry awards, including a Lifetime Achievement Award from *Romantic Times BOOKreviews* and a RITA® Award nomination from Romance Writers of America. Their books have been featured on the *USA TODAY,* Waldenbooks and B. Dalton bestseller lists. The sisters live near each other in northwestern Ohio, surrounded by children, grandchildren, brothers, sisters, aunts, uncles, cousins and old and dear friends.

To Jay Rand,
Director of Public Relations,
Homestead-Miami Speedway
In grateful appreciation
For your help and expertise

REARVIEW MIRROR:

Scandals and secrets have racked the Grosso and Murphy families for decades, starting with their longtime feud and continuing with the forbidden romance between Justin Murphy and Sophia Grosso. But nothing rivals the latest news that NASCAR driver Dean Grosso and his wife, Patsy, are on the verge of divorce. As the last race of the season approaches, the tension is high and the drama is rampant!

CHAPTER ONE

SHE'D DONE SOMETHING to her hair.

That was the first thing Dean Grosso noticed about his estranged wife as he stepped from the air-conditioned comfort of his borrowed motor home into the blazing Arizona sun. She'd cut her hair. The soft brown curls he'd always loved were gone, replaced by a sleek, sophisticated bob that swung just above her shoulders and curved against her throat. She didn't look like his Patsy-girl now. She looked like the independent and accomplished woman she was: not his wife of thirty years, not the mother of his children, not the girl he'd loved since before he was old enough to shave.

Now she was almost a stranger; a woman he'd barely spoken to, hadn't touched, hadn't woken up beside for going on five long—damned long—months.

"Hi, Patsy," he said. It would be cowardly to go back inside the motor home and pretend he hadn't seen her. The owners' and drivers' lot at every race track since they'd separated hadn't been big enough to keep them from running into each other time and again. But that didn't mean he'd gotten used to it.

"Hello, Dean," she said, her voice and manner as

calm and cool as the rest of her. "Did you have a good flight out?"

"Hit some turbulence over the Panhandle but otherwise okay. When did you get in?"

"Last night." She was carrying her usual clipboard and a leather shoulder bag, dressed in a crisply tailored beige shirt and khakis with the requisite blue-and-white Cargill Motors logo on the left pocket. She was wearing the opal studs in her ears that he'd given her on their anniversary three years ago. She didn't like big flashy jewelry. Never had. Usually just earrings, a watch, her wedding ring.

He couldn't help glancing at her left hand. No wedding ring now. It hurt, like a fist to the gut. He looked away.

"I'm on my way over to the garage to check on the car," he said, guessing she had probably already figured that out, but needing something to say. Together they owned half shares, along with his team owner and business partner, Alan Cargill, in a NASCAR Nationwide Series car and two trucks in the NASCAR Craftsman Truck Series. Even though they weren't living under the same roof, neither of them had taken any steps toward a legal separation. They were still business partners, if not husband and wife.

"That's where I'm headed, too," she admitted reluctantly.

"I'll walk with you."

"I wish you wouldn't," she said.

"I know, but it drives the gossips crazy to see us together." That got a smile out of her.

"It does confuse people."

"We might as well give them their fix for today." He took her arm and felt her muscles tense, but she turned to walk with him. "Everything looking good on the car?" he asked, dropping his hand from beneath her elbow before she could shake it off.

"Been fine-tuning the setup since they took it off the hauler. I think we're ready. Davy's due on the track in half an hour for his practice run."

Davy Andleman, the son of one of Dean's cousins, was the young driver they'd plucked from the NASCAR Craftsman Truck Series to drive the NASCAR Nationwide Series car. He hadn't won any races yet, but he had finished in the top-five three times and was improving with each race.

"Then let's go watch our investment perform."

"That reminds me, I brought some papers for you to sign."

"I'll stop by sometime and take care of it."

"Call first," she said as they climbed into his golf cart and headed for the garage area.

"Hell, Patsy, I got enough manners to do that. You don't have to be so damned cold about it."

"I know," she said, not looking directly at him. "I'm sorry I said that."

"It's okay. It's just so freakin'—" He was running out of patience with the situation he found himself in, but giving vent to his anger and frustration wouldn't do any good. It would certainly only make matters worse, maybe even push her over the edge into actually filing for divorce.

"Not now, Dean. I don't want to talk about us now. I have work to do." She fell silent while he maneuvered the golf cart through the tunnel that ran under the track. "Look, there's Kent," she said as they emerged once more into the blinding desert sunlight. The relief in her voice at no longer having to be alone with him was palpable. She waved and their son waved back, veering his cart in their direction.

"Hey, Mom. Dad," he said coming alongside them. "I didn't think I'd run in to you this soon."

"When did you get in?" Patsy responded, raising her voice as a car rumbled by on its way to the garage from its hauler. "Your motor home isn't in the lot yet."

"I'm expecting Jesse to pull in anytime. There was an accident on the interstate and he had to detour. Held him up a few hours." They wheeled the carts into a couple of parking spaces and Kent jumped out first to give his mother a hug.

"I like your hair. Makes you look—"

"Don't you dare say mature," she said with a laugh, but Dean could tell she was pleased that Kent had noticed the change.

"I was intending to say sophisticated and darned sexy. If it's okay to say that about your mother."

"It's okay," she said and gave his arm a squeeze.

Dean wanted to kick himself for not mentioning the hairstyle earlier. He didn't dare say anything now. No telling how she'd respond.

"I thought you were still in L.A.," Patsy said as they began to walk toward the garage area.

"I got out of there early, believe it or not. They'd scheduled two days for the commercial shoot but I guess I'm a natural. Got it all done in one."

"I can't wait to see it."

"I talked it over with Tanya and she decided I'd be better off coming straight here rather than fly back to North Carolina for thirty-six hours and have to deal with a double dose of jet lag."

"Sensible woman," Patsy said approvingly.

Dean approved of Kent's fiancée, too. She was smart, talented, owned her own business photographing society weddings, and she was strong enough and confident enough to handle being a NASCAR wife.

He'd always thought Patsy was the same, until this year when she'd not only demanded he retire, but when he refused to promise this season would be his last, she'd also up and walked out on him. He still couldn't get his mind around it. Still couldn't believe his thirty-year marriage was over and done. Not when he still loved her just as much as he had the day they were married.

The problem was he loved stock car racing damned near as much.

"Dad, did you hear me? I said, how's Davy coming along in the Nationwide car?"

Kent was looking at him a little quizzically, as though he'd missed a couple of beats of the conversation, which he had. He shoved his hand in the front pocket of his jeans and focused his full attention on his son.

"No wins yet but he's getting us some owner points. Wish Neely was doing as well in the truck." Neal "Neely" Andleman was Davy's brother.

"Neely's not a natural like Davy but he's a hard worker," Kent said, giving a half wave to Rafael O'Bryan, the current points leader, as he passed them in a golf cart headed for the tunnel.

Dean added a half salute of his own to his son's greeting. Kent was the reigning NASCAR Sprint Cup Series champion and Dean was as proud of that as any father on the planet. But at the moment Dean wasn't thinking like Kent's father. He was thinking like a NASCAR Sprint Cup Series driver and Rafael O'Bryan was the man standing between him and the championship title. Only sixty-seven points separated them in the Chase for the NASCAR Sprint Cup. Kent was only another thirty points behind them with only two races left to go. Dean had been racing NASCAR Sprint Cup cars for almost twenty-five years and this was the closest he'd come to the championship in a long, long time.

This year he was going to win.

But winning the championship was more than likely going to cost him any chance there might be of winning back his wife.

"KENT, I HAVEN'T HAD two minutes to talk to you in weeks," Patsy said off the top of her head to fill the silence that followed the sighting of her husband and son's biggest rival. They stood side by side, legs splayed, identical expressions on their faces, and watched the golf cart out of sight.

They were so alike, those two. Same Roman nose inherited from Dean's Italian ancestors, same head of dark brown hair, although Dean's was threaded with silver, which only made him look even more handsome in Patsy's opinion. Kent was taller than his father and he had gotten her deep blue eyes instead of Dean's dark brown ones, but there was no denying they were father and son. Their personalities were as similar as their looks: both were ambitious, focused, scrupulously fair and honest, but determined to win no matter what the cost. Including the death of a thirty-year marriage.

She didn't want to talk racing anymore. She didn't want to think about the Chase and her broken marriage. It was hard to keep her resolve when Dean was so close. She missed him. Had missed him every second of the last five, long months. But she couldn't give in. She was fighting for something important to them both. Their future. He was just too damned stubborn, too fixated on winning the NASCAR Sprint Cup championship to admit she was in the right and he wasn't. "Have you and Tanya settled on a wedding date?" she asked Kent. It was the first thought that popped into her mind because her interest in her children's lives was always percolating away just below the surface.

"Not yet," Kent admitted as they walked toward the garage area, stopping just inside the pit wall where they could still hear each other without shouting. "But we're thinking sometime just after the first of the year. Tanya has a friend who was married on this private Caribbean island—"

"Oh, Kent. How romantic. And how wonderful."

"And expensive," Dean muttered.

She turned her head to tell Dean to be quiet and stop being a penny-pincher when she realized he was teasing her, hoping to get a rise out of her. She clamped her lips shut on a retort. She no longer had the privilege of scolding him that way. Or of laughing with him. Or loving him, she thought morosely. She was his wife in name only now, and only until such time as they both retained a lawyer and began to hammer out the details of a divorce agreement.

Divorce.

The word still sounded alien to her ears. She had never, once, thought she, Patsy Clark Grosso, would ever be a divorced woman.

She'd planned since she was a little girl to love Dean Grosso until the day she died.

She still did love him. She just couldn't live with him.

"And we've kind of been waiting on Justin and Sophia," Kent said and she forced herself to stop thinking about her broken marriage and pay attention to her tall, handsome son. Kent cast Dean a slightly wary sideways look before continuing. "Is there going to be some kind of big blowout public engagement announcement when we're all in New York for Champions Week? A small family party?" He shrugged. "We don't want to steal their thunder."

"The longer we wait the better chance there is Sophia will come to her senses and leave him," Dean said, and this time he didn't smile.

Patsy sighed and held her tongue though it cost her dearly. She spent almost as much time worrying about her daughter and her secretive engagement to Justin Murphy, currently ninth in the Chase standings, and the son of Dean's old enemy, as she did about her broken marriage.

"I don't know," she admitted. "I didn't get much chance to talk to Sophia this week. It's been a zoo at the garage. I had a ton of quarterly financial reports to go over with the CPAs and Milo's got a chest cold and he's been acting like a bear with a sore paw. Nana's exhausted taking care of him."

Dean stiffened beside her and she realized he hadn't known his grandfather was ill. Like the southern gentleman he'd been raised to be, he'd moved out of the huge farm house they had shared with Dean's grandfather and his wife since Sophia left for college, and was currently staying in an apartment Cargill Motors maintained for visiting sponsor reps and such.

"Milo's not feeling well? I wondered why he wasn't at the garage Monday." Milo Grosso, one of the original generation of NASCAR drivers, and a former FBI agent who had worked with J. Edgar Hoover, was ninety-two years old. Feisty and opinionated, he was the undisputed head of the Grosso family dynasty—if you didn't count the fact that his second wife, Juliana, ruled him with a velvet fist.

"It was just the sniffles." Patsy broke her own rule and reached out to touch Dean's arm. The muscles of his hands and arms were rock-solid, as befitted a man who wrestled three thousand pounds of recalcitrant race car around the track for hours at a time. He flinched a little as her fingertips grazed the bare skin above his wrist. "He's fine, Dean. Nana bullied him into going to the doctor. Sophia went with them. He's on antibiotics and he was already feeling better before I left. I swear it."

He gave a short, sharp nod. "I'll call Nana later and check on him myself."

Patsy kept her expression neutral, not letting the sting of his abrupt dismissal show on her face. She'd had a lot of practice keeping her emotions hidden from view.

Every public figure had to perfect that skill, and NASCAR wives were no exception. "It's nearly time for practice to start. We'd better get to pit road. Coming, Kent?"

"I can't, Mom. I was on my way to a conference call when I spotted you. I'd better get a move on or I'll have some major 'splaining to do to my owner," he said in his best Ricky Ricardo imitation.

Patsy laughed as he expected her to. It had been his favorite way to coax a smile from her since he'd first learned the trick as a ten-year-old.

"Dad, I'll see you later?"

"Sure thing," Dean said and grasped Kent's upper arm with his hand. "Just FYI. I plan to be on the pole Sunday."

"What a coincidence," Kent said, returning the gesture. "So do I."

Patsy didn't respond to their exchange. She never took sides, never acknowledged their rivalry. As a wife and mother of competitive NASCAR drivers—and soon to be mother-in-law of another one—it was the only way she could keep her sanity. She gave Kent a hug and started walking toward the garage area where their car was being readied for its practice run. Dean gave Kent a single quick handshake and fell in to step beside her.

They'd barely stepped inside the building when Davy Andleman rushed up to them. His blue eyes were dark with worry and his straw-blond hair stood up in tufts on his head.

"Dean, Patsy. I'm glad to see you." He hustled them back outside again where they could hear each other.

"I have to withdraw from the race. I have to get back to Mooresville as soon as I can get on a flight." The words tumbled out of him one after the other.

Patsy put her hand on his arm. "Is it Celia?" Davy's wife was pregnant. She'd miscarried a baby the year before. She'd been having some difficulty with this pregnancy, as well.

"Yeah. She's spotting and having contractions. The doctor put her on bed rest. She's scared to death. Crying on the phone." He dragged his hand through his hair, explaining why it looked the way it did. "I'm sorry," he said. "I hate to leave you in the lurch like this but I have to get back to her. We could probably get Neely to drive for me—"

"Truck qualifying is already over. He's starting on the outside of the third row. That's his best qualifying so far this season. We'd be starting at the back of the pack if we change drivers now," Dean said.

"What about Carlton?" Their second truck was driven by Carlton Freeman, a retired journeyman NASCAR Sprint Cup Series driver, who usually produced a solid finish.

"He hasn't been in a Cup car in three years. No." Dean rubbed his hand over his chin, taking his time before he spoke, but Patsy realized he'd already made up his mind. Her heart sank.

"Don't worry about it, son. You get yourself packed up and out to the helipad." He pulled out his cell phone and began punching in numbers. "I'll call the airport and have them get the team plane ready to go."

"Thanks, Dean. I appreciate that. I...I didn't want

to have to wait for a scheduled flight but I haven't been with the team long enough to feel like I could ask—"

"Forget it," Dean said. "We're family. What's important now is that you get back to Mooresville and take care of Celia and that little one you got on the way."

Davy, looking young and scared the way he never did driving a ton-and-a-half of stock car at 160 miles an hour, pumped his older cousin's hand. "Thanks again. I…I'll keep in touch," he said. "I've got to tell Riley a couple things before I go." Riley Dunlop was their NASCAR Nationwide Series crew chief.

"Go ahead. Tell him I'll be right along to discuss what we're going to do."

"Our practice time's coming up—"

"Go," Dean insisted and Patsy felt a little jolt of pride. She'd always admired Dean's take-charge attitude. Even though it often frustrated and annoyed her to be on the receiving end of all that confident authority. "I'll drive the car."

"I knew it." Her instinct had been right. Indignation replaced the pride in his generous offer of help to the younger man. "Dean, you're too—"

"I'll drive the car," he repeated stubbornly.

"Damn you, Dean," she said despite hating airing any more of their dirty linen in front of others, even family like Davy. "You can't be serious. You're forty-nine years old. You're a dozen years older—who am I kidding?—you're twenty years older than every other driver in this garage. You're too old for this kind of stunt."

"Age has nothing to do with it. I'm not so damned old I can't drive two races in two days."

"It has everything to do with it," she said. How many times had they had this argument? "You're not as young as you used to be."

"My age has nothing to do with it. I'm going to drive the wheels off this car. And my own on Sunday." He stood with legs spread, dark eyes hidden behind mirrored sunglasses, but she had no trouble reading the anger and frustration in his expression. It matched her own. "Hell, I just might kick Neely out of his ride and drive the truck, too. Or are you going to pull rank and try and keep me out of the seat? I guess you have that right as my business partner. But not as my wife. Not any longer."

That one hurt. "Okay. Okay. Go ahead and drive yourself…to Hades," she said. "Whenever I think I might be in the wrong, might be acting selfishly, you go and pull a stunt like this. I wash my hands of you," she said, and was appalled to hear the tremor in her voice. That's what you got for mixing anger, an almost broken heart and perimenopause, an embarrassing public upheaval of emotion. A NASCAR garage was no place for tears. That had been one of the first lessons she learned when she stepped into the world of stock car racing.

"I thought you already had," he said bitterly, turned on his heel and walked away leaving her standing there clutching her clipboard to her aching heart.

CHAPTER TWO

"HEY!"

Justin Murphy looked up from the fuel consumption charts his sister Rachel had given him to study to find his fiancée, Sophia Grosso, standing in the doorway of his vintage Spartan Manor travel trailer. He blinked, wondering if she was a desert mirage, or maybe the residue of those four beers he'd consumed while playing darts with Bart and Will Branch the night before.

"Sophia?" He levered himself up from the bench-seat of the dining table and crossed the small space in two long steps to where she was standing, suitcase in hand. "What are you doing here?" He reached out to take her in his arms, finding her warm, soft curves pressed against him to be very real, and in no way, shape or form a figment of his imagination. "I thought you couldn't get away from Sunny Hills for this race."

"I have two extra personal days I forgot about," she said with her heart-stopping smile that always started just at the left corner of her mouth. "I've had my flu shot and I'm taking my vitamins. I don't intend to need those days before they run out at the end of the year. So I hitched a ride on Dad's team's plane and here I am. All ready to watch you race on Sunday."

Sophia was the director of nursing services at a large senior residential and rehabilitative complex back in Concord, North Carolina, near where they both lived. They'd agreed she wouldn't be making the trip to Phoenix with him so that she could save her remaining vacation time to attend the last race of the season in Florida, and join her family in New York City for the Champions Week festivities, where they planned to make the official announcement of their engagement. Despite the fact that most of her family, one of the most celebrated in NASCAR history, hated his guts. The feud dated back to the earliest days of the sport when his great-uncle Connor Murphy had cheated Milo Grosso out of the championship and died mysteriously a short time after. Twenty years later Justin's own father, Troy, had also died under eerily similar circumstances, ensuring the feud continued for another generation.

And then there were his own gnawing insecurities and dark thoughts that woke him in the middle of the night and kept him awake until daylight crept in through the bedroom window. Was it safe for her to marry him? Had he inherited any of his long-dead father's unsavory character traits? Would he cause her so much heartache she might lose her spirit? Or be driven to do him harm as had been the case with his Uncle Hugo's ex-wife, Sylvie.

All those thoughts and more kept him awake at night. Except those nights, which were few and far between, when she slept by his side, and he knew he would give his life, his very soul, to keep her safe and happy.

Now was one of the good times. She was beside him and he could push all the doubts aside as he took her in his arms. He couldn't help how hokey it might sound, but the world was always brighter, even here in the southwest desert where the sun seemed always to shine, when Sophia was beside him.

"I missed you," he said lowering his lips to hers. "I'm glad you came."

"I missed you, too," she said, her breath soft against his cheek, her arms tight around his neck. "I can't wait for the season to be over so that we can be together." He felt her smile. "Or at least in the same time zone."

The off-season in NASCAR was notoriously short. The last race of the year was in mid-November, and soon after Christmas and the New Year, engine tests and practice sessions began in earnest, leading up to Speed-weeks at Daytona in mid-February when the grueling thirty-six race schedule started all over again.

"Can you stay with me tonight?" he asked, stroking his hand over her sun-streaked blond hair, already knowing she probably wouldn't spend the night with him. Not with her mother and father and brother all with luxurious motor homes parked within yards of his trailer. "Please?" He kissed her again to add emphasis to his request.

"Umm," she said, kissing him back. "Don't tempt me. I can't stay with you. You know that. I'm bunking in with Kent." She stepped out of his embrace and he saw her finely arched brows pull together in a frown. "Mom's in a real tizzy because Dad's driving in the Na-tionwide race this afternoon," she said, lifting her eyes to his, pleading in her turn for his understanding. "This whole separation thing is ridiculous. My mom and dad have been in love with each other since they were kids. They've hardly ever been apart. I mean we were one of the first families to get a motor home to go to the races together. Now they're living apart and hardly speaking and both of them are miserable."

"It doesn't seem to have any effect on your dad's performance. He's been driving the wheels off his car the last couple of races."

"But that's what's keeping him and Mom apart. You know she wants him to retire, to get out from behind the wheel, spend time with her and Kent and Tanya and—"

"With you?" he said and then regretted it when he saw her blue eyes darken further.

"With the two of us," she said, squaring her jaw.

"I'm sorry, Sophia. I wasn't thinking."

"We shouldn't have to think before we mention loving each other," she said softly.

"But we do." He took her in his arms again. "At least for the foreseeable future. I don't see any signs of anyone in your family changing their mind."

"Tanya and Kent—"

"He's been civil but we're nowhere near being bosom buddies." Justin did his best to keep the his tone nonconfrontational. "There's still an outside chance I can win the championship."

"If you beat out my father and my brother in both races, you mean," she said, her frown growing more pronounced.

"It tends to put a damper on any male bonding among the three of us."

"At least Rachel seems to have accepted us as a couple."

"That's because she's in love and pregnant," Justin said.

"If your uncle, Hugo, would only acknowledge that my father and Grandpa had nothing to do with the deaths of your father and your great-uncle Connor." She took a deep shuddering breath. "It's always been just all hearsay and coincidence. That's all. I believe that with all my heart."

"I'm sorry," he said, taking her into his arms once more. "I shouldn't have brought it up. We agreed we might never learn the truth behind their deaths but that it wasn't going to come between us."

Except he had learned the truth. He knew now who was responsible for his father's hit-and-run death. Sylvie Ketchum, Hugo's ex-wife. The woman his uncle was planning to remarry after three decades. Almost thirty years earlier she'd been a frightened, traumatized nineteen-year-old that Troy Murphy had harassed to the point that she had attempted to frighten him off by trying to make him think that she was going to run over him with her truck.

The warning had worked. Too well. She had meant only to scare Troy, she swore. But at the last second he'd stepped in front of her truck. With no time to swerve she'd struck him and he died instantly. She had never told a living soul what had happened that long-ago night.

Until a few weeks ago.

And because she had donated the kidney that had saved his cousin Kim's life. And because they were both still recovering from the transplant surgery, Hugo, fearing a media firestorm if the story came out, had begged Justin and Rachel to tell no one.

Even Sophia.

Especially Sophia.

Because Justin loved Hugo, the man who had raised him from an infant, he had agreed, but the promise was taking a toll on him. And on his relationship with Sophia. He had promised her complete honesty, and instead he was telling her lies.

Sensing his agitation Sophia leaned back in his arms to study his face and he met her troubled gaze head-on, the way he'd always promised her he would, but it took every ounce of self-discipline he possessed. "You aren't your father, Justin," she assured him as though reading his mind. "You can't let those old doubts get hold of you again. Not now. Not during the Chase. You're not Troy Murphy. I love you. Hold on to that."

He didn't reply, just lowered his mouth to hers. He would try. He would try as hard as he could. But deep in his heart he wasn't sure that would be enough.

CHAPTER THREE

"ALAN! I NEVER expected to see you here." Patsy shielded her eyes from the late afternoon sun and then moved onto the rectangle of outdoor carpeting that had been laid out behind the Cargill Motors hauler. The small area, shaded by the raised tailgate of the titanic eighteen-wheeler, served as a kind of social area for Dean's team. There were folding lawn chairs, a cooler of soft drinks and a state-of-the-art grill where the hauler driver concocted meals for the largely carnivorous team members, but at the moment they had the place to themselves.

She held out her hands and the tall, white-haired team owner took them between both of his own, moving her deeper into the shade. She raised up on tiptoe and gave him a quick kiss on the cheek. "Why didn't you let us know you were going to attend the race? I can't believe you're really here." She was truly delighted to see her husband's car owner and their business partner. He had been absent from the day-to-day running of the team for far too long in her opinion.

"I decided I've spent enough time running my share of this business from a computer console and a cell phone. I wanted to see what my cars and my drivers are doing for myself."

Patsy glanced around at the empty lawn chairs lining the walkway to the hauler entrance. Not a soul to be seen, although there were usually one or two team members lolling around the area, drinking soda and talking shop. "Looks like everyone's busy getting ready for the race tonight."

"I scared them off," Alan said with a grin. "The big dog's back and no one wants to get caught sittin' down on the job." Alan Cargill, former NASCAR Sprint Cup Series champion and retired broadcaster, was in his mid-to-late sixties and looked every day of it. His skin was tanned and leathery from years of exposure to the sun and wind. His hearing had been compromised by more years of working on racing V-8s, but discreet, digital hearing aids and skill in lip reading kept his deafness from being noticeable in most situations. His smile was as broad as his shoulders and his laughter as hearty as the North Carolina tobacco-farming stock he hailed from.

"If you were looking to catch the team off guard, this was the day to do it. You haven't been to a western race…" Patsy let the sentence trail off.

"Since Caroline passed," he finished for her.

Caro Cargill had been one of her best friends. The older sister she'd never had. Patsy still missed her although she had been gone for a number of years. Alan had moved on with his life and kept company with a lovely woman named Joanna Crawford.

"Did Joanna come with you?"

"No," he said. "This trip is business, not pleasure. And it looks like I've got business to tend to. What's this I hear about my top driver putting himself behind the wheel of our Nationwide car tonight?"

"You heard right. Davy went back east to be with his wife and Dean decided, without any consultation with the rest of us, that he was going to take the ride tonight."

"I'm not sure I want him strappin' into a seat when he's going to be drivin' tomorrow. Seems like your husband should be saving his juice for the important run but Dean's too hard to argue with over the phone. It's like talking to myself."

She responded with a laugh that was halfway a sigh. "Don't I know it. You might as well pound your head against a brick wall." Dean was a man of few words. You needed to be with him to be able to read his body language and the undertones in his soft-spoken utterances to have any chance of winning an argument with him.

"If anyone can talk sense into that man, it's you."

"I intend to do my damnedest to try." Alan had stayed in the background of NASCAR the past few seasons but he wasn't ignorant of what was going on in his drivers' personal lives. "Enough of Dean. How are you holdin' up, Patsy?"

"I'm fine," she said. "I made the right decision separating from Dean, and I don't regret it for a moment."

Alan watched her for a long few seconds but she didn't let her gaze waver from his face. "Okay," he said. He pushed the brim of his big gray Stetson hat back on his head. "That's your story and you're sticking to it?"

"Yes."

"I've known you two since before the baby was taken—" He paused to take a deep breath. "Sorry, Patsy. I know how hard it is for you to talk about her."

"It was a long time ago, Alan."

"Yeah. But I haven't forgotten the little one."

"None of us have."

"But now's not the time to talk about her."

"Not today."

Alan ducked his head in agreement. "Whatever you say. But she's always in my prayers. How about coming along with me and having a bite to eat?" he asked, changing the subject. "George agreed to come out of retirement and drive my motor home. He's the second best cook on the circuit, you know, next to Kent's Jesse."

"Don't you ever let Juliana hear you say that," Patsy said, settling the strap of her leather catchall higher on her shoulder. "She's the reigning queen of NASCAR cooking and you know it."

"Heaven, how did I ever forget that?" He laughed, offering his arm. "Must be old age creeping up on me. How is Juliana and that old reprobate, Milo?"

"Milo's a bit under the weather but otherwise his old, argumentative self. I'll catch you up while we walk."

They moved briskly out into the milling crowd of race fans whose credentials dangled proudly from their necks as they gawked their way along the rows of brightly painted haulers. Team members in colored shirts and dark slacks, focused on their own business, hurried past them as they walked. Now and again the drivers in their brightly colored, sponsor-emblazoned uniforms, trailing handlers and PR reps, signed autographs as they walked, never slowing their pace.

Patsy began to relax. It would be nice to spend a quiet hour with their old friend, catch up, maybe even broach the subject of what to do with the partnership after she and Dean divorced. They were scheduled to buy Alan out, take over Cargill Motors completely, in the new year. Now, the deal—like her future—was in limbo. The last detail wasn't as pleasant to anticipate as the others and she wished it hadn't crossed her mind as a tiny, pulsing beat of pain began to drum in her temple. It intensified about a hundred times when she saw her husband walking toward them, already attired in the green-and-cream uniform of their NASCAR Nationwide Series car's sponsor.

"There's Dean," Alan said unnecessarily. "Already dressed to drive it looks like."

"Yes." Patsy sighed, tension coiling back into her body, tightening her nerves. "I can't seem to avoid running into him for more than fifteen minutes at a time."

WHAT WAS IT about this place? Dean checked up for half a stride. He'd run in to Patsy more often in the last forty-eight hours than he had at any of the three races before it. He wished he just didn't get that punched-in-the-gut feeling every time it happened. He could feel a frown pulling his brows together and made himself relax. Damn, if he could just get used to seeing her out on her own like this it would be a lot easier.

"Alan! It's true. You are here," he said. He enclosed Alan's right hand in his own and gave it a hearty shake, ignoring Patsy for the moment, and damned proud he could do it. "I didn't believe you when you said you were flying out here to knock some sense into me."

"I intend to do just that." Alan wasn't smiling quite as

broadly, Dean noticed with just a bit of unease. He and Alan Cargill had been friends for more than half his life, but Alan was still the car owner, still his boss—at least until the first of the year. If the deal went through, that was.

"I wouldn't be driving tonight if I didn't think it was necessary," Dean said, repeating the explanation he'd given Alan over the phone the day before.

"We've got other drivers," Alan responded. "You're within striking distance of the lead for the NASCAR Sprint Cup championship. Why take a chance?"

"Because it's my car, too," Dean said, knowing he sounded surly but suddenly too angry to care. What in hell was wrong with everyone? He was forty-nine years old. Not ninety-nine. He was at the top of his game. He could drive two races in two days without collapsing— and he intended to.

He opened his mouth to say just that then thought better of it. There were people all around them. Standing still in one spot had already started attracting a crowd. A couple of hero cards were thrust in his face. Automatically he accepted the marker the fan handed him and scribbled his signature, smiling and exchanging pleasantries with only a small fraction of his attention.

Out of the corner of his eye he saw a pit reporter from one of the cable networks spot them and veer off in their direction. Alan saw the man, conspicuous in a white driver's uniform emblazoned with his network's logo, too, and began urging Patsy forward.

"We'll talk later, Dean," Alan said, slipping his hand under Patsy's elbow just the way Dean had done the day before. But this time his wife made no move to shrug off her escort. Anger and something deeper and darker—jealousy maybe?—began to knot the muscles at the back of his neck. Alan Cargill was twenty years older than Dean but he was still a man and Dean didn't like him having his hands on Patsy one bit. "But not until I've had something to eat. Patsy's been gracious enough to agree to join me. I don't want to spoil my appetite, and give the press a show by reaming you a new one out here in front of everyone. I'll see you in the hauler later."

"If we were talking Smoothtone business here," Dean said quietly but with just as much steel in his voice as his old friend and mentor. "I'd be there waiting when you walked in the hauler. But we're not. We're talking my car here, just as much as it's yours."

"Our car," Patsy interrupted in that cool, dismissive tone he hated. "Don't forget that."

"I'm not forgetting anything," he said, glad he was wearing the reflective sunglasses he'd made his trademark. He didn't want her to see the hurt beneath the anger, and she knew him far too well not to notice it. "I'm driving this race. That's all there is to say about it."

Alan shoved his big Stetson back on his head. "Okay. That's enough. We're not givin' these people any more show. We'll talk later. About you drivin' and about where Cargill-Grosso Racing is going. Agreed?"

"Agreed," Dean growled out between clenched teeth. He'd let his jealousy get the better of him and now, just like a rookie, he was getting a set down from one of the men he admired most in the world. "But I'm driving tonight and that's the end of it."

"Hell, Dean. What's gotten in to you? You're even more damned stubborn than you used to be, boy. I don't blame this woman one damned bit for walking out on you."

"THAT'S THE WAY he's been the entire season," Patsy said, picking at her apple walnut salad as they sat in the dining area of Alan's motor home. It was an older model, but filled with comfortable furniture and mellow wood in the creams and earthtones that Caro had loved. "Completely unreasonable. I can't have an intelligent civilized conversation with him that doesn't end in an argument in less than five minutes' time. That's why I left him. I couldn't live like that any longer."

"He's always been headstrong, Patsy. You've had worse things than this happen and you got through them together. Why is it so different now?"

She looked up, ashamed to find tears pushing at the corners of her eyelids. "I don't know why it's different now. It just is. Maybe it's my age. Maybe it's because I remember how it used to be. When we were partners in every aspect of our lives, as well as husband and wife. We talked things over. We made decisions together. Then it all ended. It all came apart." She pushed her plate away. "So quickly. And so completely. I wonder how long I was fooling myself that he still loved me?"

Alan gave a snort of exasperated laughter. "Good Lord, Patsy. Don't go all dramatic on me. You two have argued as long as I've known you. And loved each other for longer than that. Don't go blamin' your troubles on a lack of communication. Sounds like you've been watching one of those TV psychologists. What's really bothering you?"

She didn't feel like crying any more, but she did feel suddenly foolish and melodramatic. "I want him to retire," she said, "but he won't hear of it."

"He's in his prime," Alan stated after a short hesitation.

Patsy rolled her eyes. "He's forty-nine. He's got twenty-five years on the younger drivers. He's an old man in a young man's sport."

"He's only sixty points out of first place with two races to go. He may have the years on those young guns but he's also got the experience to go with them."

"I don't want him to win the championship," Patsy said bluntly. "Whatever chance we might have of getting back together will disappear if that happens."

"How do you know that?"

"Because if he wins he'll never give up driving. He'll keep going until he's too old and arthritic to climb in the car or until you take his ride away."

Alan held up a hand. "Whoa, Patsy, Dean's got a ride with me as long as he wants it—" Alan paused and narrowed his eyes "—and as long as he's winning races." He raised his hand, palm out. "I'll talk to him if you want me to but I doubt it will help. This is something you're going to have to solve between the two of you."

"That's just the problem, Alan," Patsy said emphatically, pushing away another wave of self-pity and concentrating on the anger just thinking of her stubborn husband kindled within her. "He isn't going to change his mind. And neither am I."

A knock at the door of the motor home prevented Alan from responding to her last defiant statement. He got up and opened the door. "Sophia. Honey, you're a sight for sore eyes, you are. Come on in here. Your mother and I were just having a bite of lunch."

"Hi, Uncle Alan. I can't believe you're here." Patsy smiled as her daughter sailed into the motor home. Sophia threw her arms around Alan and gave him a fierce hug. "I've missed you. I couldn't believe it when I saw George wheel your motor home into the lot."

"It's good to be back. But aren't you a wee bit past your usual stompin' grounds this far west, too?"

A slight blush tinged Sophia's cheeks. She gave Patsy a half glance. "I…I've been attending a few more races this season. Dad's so close to winning the championship that it's hard to stay home and not be here to cheer him on."

"Your dad's season isn't the only reason for you bein' here though, is it?" he asked, holding both her hands and taking a step back to better gauge her reaction. Once more Sophia shot her a half-apologetic glance and Patsy's heart squeezed a little bit. It was another sore point between her and Dean—Sophia's unwelcome involvement with Justin Murphy. She wanted her daughter to be happy, and if her happiness lay with the son of Dean's old enemy then she would swallow all her resentment and welcome him into the family circle for her daughter's sake. But not Dean. Not yet. Probably not ever.

Sophia's blush deepened. "Well, there is someone else I'm rooting for. Justin Murphy."

"The Murphy boy? Gonna be a damned fine driver

if he ever gets it all together. Seems to me I remember he had some bad luck the middle of the season but his team pulled it together and got him into the Chase. Where's he standin' now?"

"Ninth," Sophia said. "But he's going to move up in the standings tomorrow. I'm sure of it."

Alan laughed. "You sound just like your mother, young woman. Always talking up your brother and your dad." He ground to a halt and coughed to cover his lapse.

"I'm Kent's mother so what do you expect?" Patsy stood up from the leather banquette, coming to his rescue. "And I'm Dean's business partner so I'm not going to stop rooting for him just because I can't live with the man." She moved past Alan to give her daughter a quick hug. "Sophia? Do you want to watch the race tonight from our pit stall?"

Once more Sophia hesitated just a moment, as though weighing her words before she spoke them, and once more the niggling pain squeezed Patsy in the region of her heart. "I'm going to watch the race tonight with Justin. It…it would probably be best if we watched from the top of his hauler, if that's all right. I don't want to upset Dad."

Patsy snorted. "You know how he is once he straps himself in to the car. He probably won't even notice whether we're there or not. All his attention's on the car and his driving."

"That's the way it should be, Patsy," Alan admonished her quietly. "Anything less than total concentration could take him out of the race."

"I know that, Alan. We've been separated for months

and it hasn't even made it into the papers yet. I'm not going to do anything to make a spectacle of myself. But the season's over in less than ten days. Then all bets are off. Whether he wins the championship or not Dean and I are getting a divorce unless he promises to give up driving."

CHAPTER FOUR

THE NASCAR NATIONWIDE SERIES races, although a step below the NASCAR Sprint Cup Series races, were still as adrenaline-fueled and testosterone-heavy, attracting NASCAR Sprint Cup drivers as well as serving as a training ground for up-and-coming NASCAR stars.

Patsy just wished her husband wasn't one of those double-dipping drivers.

But she had learned not to wish for what she couldn't have many, many years before. She had told Alan she was divorcing Dean after the end of the season unless he quit racing. She had seen the shocked look on Sophia's face when the words came tumbling out of her mouth and wondered if her daughter's reaction hadn't been mirrored in her own expression. Was she really that committed to spending the rest of her life alone, waking up alone? Going to sleep alone, growing old alone?

Had she really meant it? Was she going to walk away from her thirty-year marriage, thirty-year love affair, without another glance. Did she have the guts to do that?

She didn't know. But she did know she didn't have the courage to stay in a marriage any longer where she wasn't certain what the next day, the next hour, even the next minute might bring. That burden was for women younger and less fearful of what the future held.

The way she had always used to be.

"Gentleman, start your engines."

The roar of thousands of horsepower roaring to life not more than fifty feet from where she was sitting startled her out of her reverie. She shook her head. *Reverie* was too kind a word for the hamster wheel of what-ifs and if-onlys that kept her mind in almost constant turmoil these days.

She looked down at the scoreboard in her hand. Low-tech and old-fashioned, along with the stopwatch Milo had given her when Dean got his first NASCAR Sprint Cup ride, it still served well to keep a running tally of her driver's speed and lap times.

Dean's voice came over the microphone embedded in her protective headset. "Ready to rock and roll, guys?" he asked Davy's team.

"Ready, boss," came their crew chief's response.

Dean laughed and Patsy felt her toes curl. She loved his laugh. "You're the boss, tonight, Riley," he replied. "I'm just drivin' the car."

"I'll remember that when you start callin' the race from the back straightaway," Riley retorted.

"Ready on the box?" he asked.

Patsy's mouth went dry and she couldn't answer. She kept her eyes fixed on her clipboard knowing that Kent, who was sitting beside her, was watching her. She didn't want their son to see the confusion in her eyes so she didn't raise her head.

Kent touched her hand. "Is your radio working?" he asked.

She took the coward's way out.

"What?" She tapped the big protective earphones. "Okay now," she said, forcing a smile to her stiff lips. She hadn't walked Dean to his car for the pre-race ceremonies, she hadn't shared a moment of prayer as they always did, but it hadn't seemed so unusual at the time. She was an owner and part of the team for these races, not just Dean's adoring and supportive wife, her role for tomorrow's race. But now she regretted her stubbornness. Now that it was too late, but still the words wouldn't come.

Thankfully Kent answered for her. "Ready to rock and roll. Good luck," he said, giving his father a thumbs-up, although Dean couldn't see the gesture from where he was, a hundred yards away, on the inside of the tenth row.

"Patsy-girl, aren't you going to wish me luck?" he asked in his husky, still sexy voice.

"Good luck," she whispered, but not loudly enough for it to be caught by the microphone because her throat was clogged with emotion she didn't dare let show. And then the pace car moved out onto the track leading its colorful kite's tail of race cars and the moment was lost.

THIRTY LAPS left to race and there were only two cars ahead of him. He'd found a groove and he was going to ride it for as long as he could. He really ought to just lay back here in the weeds and finish in the money. That would be the smart way to race, the prudent way. But he was done with being prudent and smart. For twenty-five seasons he'd followed that path and what did he have to show for it? His best season finish ever was second and that was a long, long time ago. Back in the day, as the TV announcers always said.

He wanted it all now. This might be his last season. It might be his last race. You never knew.

His spotter cautioned him to watch out for one of the lapped cars, which had a piece of sheet metal flapping on the rear bumper. He didn't want that coming loose landing on the track in front of him and shredding a tire. Dean continued driving, passing the damaged car with its rookie driver and lining up to pass yet another lapped car, when ahead of him a telltale plume of smoke signaled a blown engine on one of the lead cars. And then, in the blink of an eye, in less time than it took his brain cells to fire, cars began sliding every which way as oil sprayed from the damaged vehicle. Dean heard his spotter hollering directions into his microphone, began acting on the orders without consciously hearing them.

"Stay low. Stay low. Keep going. Keep going." Total trust: it was essential at this point as he drove blindly into a choking cloud of acrid smoke. Untouched, he and the car came out the other side in one piece, but then his luck failed. The car beside him got loose, fishtailed up the track and smacked the outside wall, careening back down the banked turn, T-boning him directly in the passenger side door, or what would have been the passenger side door on an ordinary car.

The impact came like a brick wall in his face. It all happened too fast for him to get off the gas, and get on the brake. The HANS device that protected his neck and shoulders did its job and he held on to the wheel as his car bucked and jolted, locked in a dizzying dance as they skidded onto the infield grass. His race car hit the safety wall where the other car clocked around and came to rest on the apron, while Dean continued to slide along the concrete barrier, scattering fans and emergency workers and finally coming to a halt just short of the entrance to pit road.

He sat for a moment, already aching in every bone and muscle, and assessed the damage, first to himself— hard hit but nothing serious—and then to his car. Not so good there. Lots of side damage, lots of torn sheet metal and leaking fluids and the smell of hot rubber. No smoke though, just steam from a broken hose. He could take a moment to get his breath before climbing out of the window. He unhooked the netting that had kept his head and arms inside and raised his hand in salute so the fans and emergency workers knew he was okay. He popped the heavy safety harness that held him in his seat and heaved himself through the open window. He stood there a moment, getting his balance, waiting for the emergency crews to arrive, surveying the damage to his car, admitting to himself for the first time that maybe Patsy was right. Maybe he was too old for this.

"YOU RIDICULOUS MAN. Why did you get back in the car and finish the race?" He'd never been so happy to be scolded by her before. At least it meant she was here beside him. In his motor home, or more technically, Cargill's VIP motor home, but who cared where they were. They were alone. Together. For the first time in weeks and weeks.

"It wasn't that bad a wreck." They'd changed out the

front end during the long caution that followed the wreck and he'd gone back out on the track to finish fifteenth. Not bad considering the shape the car was in. "And besides," he added stubbornly, "we need the owner points."

"Do you think I care about owner points?" she scolded, pacing back and forth in front of him. She'd been there in the small private waiting area of the infield care center when they'd turned him loose, just as she'd been every time he'd been taken there over the years. Smiling and upbeat, her hand cold and clammy in his as they walked out of the building into the holding area where the track officials and the press were congregated, she'd kept her emotions to herself and charmed the hell out of them all as usual. But he'd sensed the tension beneath the calm exterior, the sense that she wasn't done with him that night, and sure enough, when he'd finally made it back to the motor home an hour after the race ended, there she was waiting for him.

"What are you doing here?" he'd asked, wanting nothing more than to stand under a hot shower and then fall into bed.

"Old habits die hard," she'd replied, turning away from the sink with a glass of water in one hand and a couple of the extra-strength over-the-counter pain medication he endorsed in the other. "Here. You probably need these." He wanted to tell her he sure as hell didn't need them, but he couldn't voice the lie.

"Thanks," he said and swallowed them both.

"I'll fix you a sandwich while you're in the shower."

"You don't have to do that."

"I'm hungry, too," was all she said, as she turned her back and stuck her head in the open refrigerator door.

He'd half expected to find the sandwich wrapped in plastic in the refrigerator and her gone when he got out of the shower but he'd been wrong. They ate in silence and she cleaned off the table while he finished his drink, but she made no effort to hurry away and he was happy to have her stay.

He wondered if he could talk her into staying the night? Their love life had always been good; they always ended their squabbles in the bedroom. Could they still come together that way now? Sadly, he doubted it. He reached up to rub the back of his neck. The muscles were so tight he could feel them knotted like ropes beneath his skin.

"Here," she said impatiently, "let me do that." She kicked off her shoes and moved across the carpet barefoot. She had pretty feet, long and narrow, and always with some surprising color of polish on the nails. Tonight it was neon pink, far more bright and youthful than the pale pink on her fingernails and lips.

She knelt beside him on the sofa as he angled his body toward the window, away from the sight of her slender feet and her rounded body. He ached all over, inside as much as outside. *God, he missed her.* Every minute of ever day, and night, too. Her hands on his skin were firm and cool. Her attitude, and her voice, matched her touch. "You have no business driving tomorrow," she said.

He sighed. He couldn't hide his weariness from her so he didn't try. He reached up and circled her wrist with his fingers. "Enough." He couldn't endure anymore of her emotionless touch. "I'll be fine tomorrow. I'm fine now." He tugged her down beside him, folding his arms around her although his bruised ribs protested the sudden movement. "All I've ever needed to feel like I was on top of the world was to have you in my arms." He pressed his mouth to hers although she pushed against his chest with both hands, holding her body away from him.

He didn't tighten his grip, although he longed to crush her against him and never let her out of his arms again. He let his mouth play over hers, softly, beseechingly, tasting the softness of her mouth, urging her to part her lips and let his tongue inside. For a while she resisted him and he almost gave up in despair, pulled back to let her move away from him, but he persisted and slowly, by increments, she yielded to the old magic that had always flared between them when they kissed.

"I miss you," he whispered against her cheek when the kiss ended and she clung to him and he to her. "I miss you every night and every morning. I want you back. I want you here with me together just like we've been since we were ten. That's when I knew you were the one for me. You're still the one. I love you, Patsy-girl."

She tilted her head back and watched him from blue eyes dark with emotion, as unreadable as the carvings on some ancient stone tablet. "I've never doubted you love me, Dean. That's not our problem."

He reached out and smoothed his fingers over the sleek fall of hair by her ear. It had always been soft and curling to his touch, now it was silky and clung to his fingers like gossamer strands. "Our problem is me, isn't it?" he said, wanting more than anything to kiss her again, to scoop her up in his arms and carry her into the bedroom and make love to her, communicating through lovemaking all the things it was so hard for him to put into words.

"Yes," she said. "And don't even think of it. I'm not going to bed with you." She raised her hands and framed his face. "I always lose arguments we take into the bedroom. Once you have me in bed I forget whatever it is was I was mad at you about. But this time it's too important to me to lose track of myself."

"It's worked for thirty years," he said, smiling ruefully.

She straightened, gave her head a little shake. "It's not going to work this time. This is too serious. It means too much to me, Dean. It's our future. It's my peace of mind. I'm afraid. I'm afraid all the time now. I don't want to go on without you but if I have to it's going to be because it was my choice and not fate's."

"Do we have to go through this again?" he asked, suddenly angry with her. Why couldn't she understand how important finishing the season, winning the championship, was to him. It was a goal he'd thought they'd always shared. Now she was dismissing it as though it was no more important than if he worked for Smoothtone Music or one of his other sponsors and he was trying to decide if he should retire after twenty-five years or go for thirty.

"Yes," she said, her voice a little softer as she lifted her eyes to his once more. "Until I get some kind of response from you that I can understand."

He released her and splayed his hands on his knees,

looking down at the floor. "What's not to understand? I'm going to drive tomorrow. I'm going to drive next week. I'm aiming to win the championship and if I do I'm going to come back and defend the title. I know that's not what you want to hear but it's the only answer I've got."

"I figured as much." She sounded resigned and sad. "But I had to give it one more try. I'll be—"

"DAD? YOU IN THERE?" It was Kent's voice coming from outside the door.

"Stay put. I'll let him in," Patsy said, oddly relieved that their son's arrival had put an end to the massage and prevented her from finishing her ultimatum. Surely Dean knew what she'd intended to say. That she'd be hiring a divorce lawyer as soon as she got back to Concord. But saying the words aloud had been harder than she'd planned.

"Hi, Dad. How are you feeling?" Sophia entered the motor home just ahead of her brother, Alan Cargill bringing up the rear. The desert sun had brought out her freckles and reddened the tip of her nose. She was wearing a Smoothtone Music jacket and her sun-streaked blond hair was pulled through the back of a Vittles Farm ball cap, Kent's sponsor. No Turn-Rite Tools gear could be seen on her person though, and as always Patsy felt a pang of sadness that her daughter had to keep her feelings for Justin Murphy hidden away when she was around the rest of the family.

"How do you think I feel? Like I hit a concrete wall at a hundred and fifty miles an hour," Dean said, enfolding Sophia in his arms. "I'm fine. Stiff and sore but

I'll be in the car when the flag drops tomorrow. Alan, come in. Can I get you a beer?"

"Maybe later," the older man replied, taking off his big gray Stetson and holding it between his hands.

"Have a seat, Alan," Dean said. "Everyone. Sit down."

"I...I have to be going." There was no way Patsy could stay and make small talk any longer. She had a pounding headache. She wanted peace and quiet and her own bed.

Sophia glanced in her direction. Patsy raised her shoulders and gave a weary shrug that said *I'm done arguing with him.* She sat down on the couch and dragged on her shoes, determined that her children and her old friend would not see the tears that suddenly pricked at the corners of her eyes.

"We just stopped by to check on Dad," Kent inserted smoothly.

"I met them outside," Alan added.

"Nana called and Grandpa is back to his old self. They're thinking of coming to Homestead next week," Sophia explained.

"Fantastic. I wanted to call them after the race but it was too late by the time I got out of the media center," Dean said, a frown between his brows.

"I talked to Nana," Sophia informed her father. "They didn't know you were driving in the Nationwide race. She was, um—" She looked down at her shoes for a moment, considering her choice of words.

"Nana was p.o.'d," Kent offered.

"I'll bet she was," Alan said, grinning.

"She said to tell you you're too old to double up on

races and if she'd been here she would have told you so to your face."

Alan laughed out loud. Dean's face reddened. Patsy held her breath, then let it out again in a soundless sigh when his frown smoothed into a smile. "I figured as much. What did Milo say?"

"He's glad you finished. You need the points."

Dean shook his head, still grinning. "Also what I expected."

"And there's a message from Davy, too. Carrie's fine. The contractions and spotting have stopped. She's on bed rest but he says to tell you he'll be ready to race next weekend. That is, if he's got a car."

"Okay. My good humor only stretches so far," Dean growled. "How about getting us those beers, Kent?"

"Sounds good. Mom, can I fix you a nightcap?"

"No. I've stayed too long as it is." Kent winced. She hadn't meant the words to sound so loud or so harsh. She lowered her voice and softened her tone. "I'll see you all at the drivers' meeting tomorrow. Good night, Alan. Good night, Dean."

"Good night, Patsy." He might have been bidding a fan "good evening" for all the emotion evident in his voice.

"I'll walk with you, Mom," Sophia said. "I'm tired, too, it's been a long day."

They left and walked back between the rows of large motor homes toward the one Patsy and Dean had shared for the past four seasons. It wasn't terribly late, only a little after eleven, but many of them were already dark. Race days were long and grueling and most drivers and their families turned in early the night before.

"Are you okay, Mom?" Sophia asked, linking arms.

"I'm fine," Patsy replied automatically. Sophia was a worrier. She always had been, even as a child. There had been a time over the last few years when she seldom came to the races. She always had an excuse, work or commitments to friends, or staying behind with Juliana and Milo when they didn't care to travel to distant race tracks. Patsy had always known what the true reason was for all those excuses. Sophia was afraid for her father and her brother.

But since the beginning of this season, when she had become reacquainted with Justin Murphy after the first race at Daytona and fallen in love with him, she'd been around a lot more. Her love had given her new courage, and Patsy was glad that had happened. Glad that Sophia and Justin were able to stand up to the barrage of negativity that came at them from his family as well as hers.

"Where's Justin?" Patsy asked as they walked through the chilly darkness. It was one of the things she couldn't get used to about racing in this desert climate. By day the sun beat down mercilessly from an achingly blue sky, but when the sun dropped behind the low range of mountains to the west the air turned cool in a matter of minutes. It was nothing like the moist, clinging heat of the Carolinas, where she'd been born and raised.

And where she'd always assumed she and Dean would settle down and grow old together.

Except of course Dean wouldn't hear of retiring.

Her anger level spiked again. She didn't want to sit on the porch on summer nights, drinking sweet tea, listening to the crickets and watching lightning bugs flicker over the meadow while she fanned herself and complained about the heat alone, damn it. She wanted that stubborn man there by her side until they were as old as Milo and Juliana.

"He's turning in early. He has a team meeting scheduled first thing in the morning," Sophia was saying and Patsy forced her attention back from her ongoing inner argument with herself. "He's so focused on this race it's as if he's not even in the room with me sometimes."

"They're all like that come race time," Patsy reminded her. "Especially when the championship's on the line."

"Kent isn't. He's always willing to listen to me if I need a sympathetic ear, even if it's only a couple of hours until the race starts."

"You're his baby sister. He's always been there to take care of you. If you asked Tanya what he was like before a race I'm positive you'd get a different answer."

Sophia sighed. "I suppose you're right." Her gaze strayed off to the row of luxury motor homes where Justin's vintage travel trailer gleamed dully in their shadows. "We see the side of them they don't want the public to be aware of, don't we?"

"A super hero without his cape," she said dryly. "The up-close-and-personal, warts-and-all side." Patsy was annoyed the bitterness had managed to seep back into her tone.

Sophia stopped walking a moment. "Are you and Dad really going through with a divorce?" she asked. It was the first direct question on their faltering marriage she'd received from her daughter. She hated the pain and anxiety she could see reflected in Sophia's eyes even in the darkness, but she couldn't—wouldn't— lie to her.

Answering required another deep breath. "Yes, I am."

"I…I'd hoped when Kent and I saw you together in Dad's motor home that—well, maybe?"

"We were reconciling? I'm afraid not. I was just making sure he was all right. I was worried when he hit the wall."

They stopped at the doorway of her motor home. Sophia wrapped her arms around herself as though to ward off the chill of the desert night. "He still loves you, Mom. You know that, don't you? Why can't you work things out?"

"Because he's stubborn and opinionated and he won't listen to a word I say."

"He wants to win the championship more than anything."

"And I want to travel and see the great museums of Europe and wiggle my toes in the sand on a beach in Tahiti, and maybe take a cruise up the Amazon. But I don't want to do all that alone, do you understand?"

"You're afraid just like me, aren't you?"

Sophia wasn't a child any longer. She deserved the truth. "Yes, I am. Afraid for him and for myself. Now that you and Kent are both considering marriage I've been thinking of what it will be like to be a grandmother. And I want to share lovin' those grandbabies you two will give us with their grandfather, not my memories of him."

"Dad's one of the best drivers in the business. Don't make him choose between you and his driving, Mom."

"He's already made his choice," Patsy said, horrified to hear a telltale catch in her voice. "He's chosen racing. Not me."

Welcome to real-life drama, Riley said, her voice low enough to reach only to her ears. "It's always like this. Nonstop . . ."

CHAPTER FIVE

JUSTIN COULDN'T SLEEP. Even though his internal clock kept telling him it was late back home in North Carolina, here in Phoenix it was the "shank of the evening," as the old-timers used to say.

He wanted Sophia. He wanted her to lay with him in the big bed that took nearly all the floor space at the back of the trailer. He wanted to hold her in his arms and listen to her breathing, be warmed by the heat of her body, be lulled into sleep by the scent of her hair and her skin.

He stood in the darkness of the kitchen area and looked out of the wraparound windows at the sleeping lot. Where was she? What was she doing? He could call her on his cell but even after eight months of being together he still hesitated to do that when he knew she was with her family.

She felt the same, he knew. She never called when he was at the garage, or if she suspected he would be in the hauler with his sister, Rachel, and his uncle, Hugo, close by.

He opened the door and stepped down into the darkness. His vintage travel trailer, thirty-five feet long from tail to hitch, was dwarfed by the fifty-foot motor homes on either side. He rested a hand on the shining aluminum skin. One more cross-country trip for the old girl, a weekend in Florida and then a well-earned retirement on a knoll overlooking Lake Norman.

He'd already picked out a motor home for next season. Not a million-dollar unit like Kent Grosso's or Rafael O'Bryan's, but one that would put him in the same league as the other up-and-coming drivers, and one that would be just right for a newly married couple.

He had given his word to Hugo to keep Sylvie's secret until she was ready to reveal it to Sophia and the rest of the Grossos, but how much longer would that be? How much longer would he have to go on lying to the woman he loved, while the unrelieved animosity between the feuding families put their future at risk?

The sound of footsteps and feminine voices whispered to him on the desert wind. He took another couple of steps and saw the outlines of two women stop in front of Patsy Grosso's motor home. The women were the same height and nearly the same build. It took him only a moment to recognize his fiancée and her mother. They remained heads close together and continued speaking for another minute or two. Justin stayed where he was, out of sight, out of earshot.

Patsy was less antagonistic toward his relationship with her daughter than Dean Grosso was, but it was still awkward. Sophia's mother wouldn't be happy to know he was lurking in the shadows, waiting for her to go inside so that he could intercept Sophia before she reached her brother's motor home.

He wanted her with him, at least for a little while, not tucked up, alone, inside yet another of the seemingly limitless number of motor homes the Grosso family owned or had access to. Patsy's shadowy figure entered her motor home and the door closed behind her. Sophia turned to go into Kent's, which was parked nearby. Justin left the shadows and sprinted across the paved roadway. He reached out and took Sophia by the hand. The suddenness of his movement startled her and she let out a squeak of alarm.

"Shh, it's me," he growled, pulling her into his embrace. Her heart was pounding rapidly beneath the thin cotton of her shirt.

"Justin, you scared me half to death," she said, her forehead pressed against his shoulder. She lifted her face. "Don't ever do that again," she admonished, but he felt her smile.

"I'm sorry," he said, dropping a quick kiss on her cheek and a longer, more satisfying one on her mouth as he maneuvered them into the deeper shadows beneath the awning of Kent's motor home. "I just wanted to catch you before you got inside and your brother closed the drawbridge."

"He's not here. He's with Dad," she said. "Alan Cargill's there, too. He's worried about Mom and Dad." And possibly about the deal for Dean and Patsy to buy Cargill Motors falling through, Justin thought, but didn't say aloud.

"I haven't seen you since the race ended."

She shuddered. "I've been talking on the phone with Grandad and Nana. Seeing Dad wreck upset them both. Me, too."

He tightened his arms and kissed her again, hoping to coax her out of her dark mood. She returned his kiss and let her lips linger on his, but she was still tense in his arms. He lifted his head and stared down into her eyes.

He held her slightly away from him. "Will you walk me to my car tomorrow?" he asked. It was the way they'd announced the seriousness of their relationship to their families, to the whole NASCAR world at the spring Bristol race.

She closed her eyes and a frown appeared between her softly arched eyebrows. "Justin, I—"

"What, Sophia?" He knew the continued antipathy between their families was taking its toll on her, corroding their happiness, weakening her resolve. He knew the Grossos were still actively agitating to have her break off their not-yet-formalized engagement. His stomach clenched. How much longer could they go on like this before they ended up estranged the way Patsy and Dean Grosso had become?

"I wonder if we shouldn't take a break?"

He shut his eyes for a moment, fighting a burst of pain and dark anger. Control. He had to control his emotions. This was too important to let adrenaline overtake common sense. "We'll be getting a break soon," he promised. "Two more races and the season's over. We'll have time to set both our families down. Let them know we're not going to let bad blood between our families keep us apart."

"The season will be over but you know it will still be hectic. There's Thanksgiving and then Champions Week in New York, and Christmas and New Year's and Kent and Tanya's wedding, and then you'll be back in Daytona testing for next year. I just don't see—" She stopped talking, out of breath.

It was a daunting schedule but he was fighting for their happiness, their future. He wasn't going to give in.

"We'll make time. I'll kidnap them all one at a time if I have to. Lock them in a room together." And tell them what? *I know none of you were responsible for my SOB father's death, but I can't tell you who was. But, hey? What's a little vehicular homicide between friends and family? And, oh, yeah, Milo, are you sure, being ninety-two and all, that you maybe didn't just forget you might have run my great-uncle Connor off the side of a mountain fifty-odd years ago?*

Sophia's thoughts were following a different line. "I can't even get my father and mother to sit down at the dinner table together." She gave a shuddering little laugh.

He ignored his own doubts to keep hers at bay. "Hell, Sophia. Don't start going wobbly on me now. We've faced them down for the last eight months. We're close now." She opened her mouth as though to protest but he kept on talking. "Wade and Rachel are on our side, and Hugo will come around, I promise you. Now that he's back together with Kim's birth mother he'll have to recognize that our love is at least as strong as what they feel for each other." Lord, he prayed he was right, that Hugo would release him from a promise he'd made when they were all worried that Kim and Sylvie might not survive the transplant procedure.

She reached out and put her hands on his arms. "Don't you see, Justin? It's me. I'm afraid again. How will we ever make a go of our marriage if my parents can't? I always thought they had the perfect marriage, but now they can't even be in the same room together without arguing. My mother is hiring a lawyer. She's going to divorce my father after all the years they've spent together."

"You don't know that for sure. When the season's over—"

"For men like you and my dad and my brother the season's never over. That's what I'm afraid of now. That I will lose you and never get you back."

CHAPTER SIX

SHE OUGHT TO BE a happy woman, Patsy thought to herself as she stared out the window of her small second-floor office that overlooked the main garage area of Cargill Motors. As always the floor gleamed white and pristine, clean enough to eat off of. Men, and a few women in dark slacks and Cargill blue shirts, moved around the big, brightly lit space, clipboards in hand. Some labored on one or another of the No. 414 car chassis that were parked in various work bays. To an outsider the garage didn't look particularly busy. That's because all of the important work went on in an area of the building that fans and outsiders were not allowed to see.

Racing was big business and as in any competitive enterprise there were spies everywhere—at least to hear Alan Cargill tell it. Only the most basic body and engine work went on in the open where fans and the occasional VIP tour could watch from a fenced-in viewing area. But for most of them it didn't matter. They were where the action was. They took photographs and videos of the car chassis, the employees, the massive, tiered red toolboxes aligned along the white, cinderblock walls and, most often of all, the colorful sponsor banners and heroic-sized likenesses of Dean and the other Cargill drivers suspended from the high ceiling, staring down at visitors and employees alike, their expressions stern, their emotions hidden behind mirrored sunglasses.

Accusing, Patsy thought. Judgmental.

She swiveled her chair back to face her computer screen. She'd been staring at the same spreadsheet for the last fifteen minutes and it still didn't make sense to her. She exited out of the program and leaned her head against the back of the chair. What was she going to do with her life if she went through with her threat to divorce Dean?

Would she have to leave NASCAR? Or could she take her half of their assets and buy in to another team? Start her own?

A wry smile tugged at her lips. No way. She and Dean had done well in life. He had made wise choices on endorsements, and she had invested his prize money well over the years, taking courses in accounting and finance and economics until she was only a few credits from her degree. If he retired they would be comfortably well off but far from rich.

But rich was what it took to own a NASCAR team. Competing at a NASCAR Sprint Cup Series level was big business these days. Multimillion-dollar business. Starting her own team was out of the question. And the divorce settlement, no matter how equitable, would force them both to renege on their agreement to buy Cargill Motors—now possibly never to be known as Cargill-Grosso Racing, the name they'd chosen before the separation—from Alan in the new year.

She swiveled her head at the sound of a knock on her door. The silhouette of a man was outlined in the frosted glass. *Dean*. She squelched an impulse to lift her hand to her hair to make sure each strand was in place. She wondered for the fleeting second she allowed the thought to surface, if he liked what she had done to it? "Come in," she said, clearing her throat before she spoke.

He stuck his head around the door. "Hi. Can I have a minute of your time?"

"Of course," she said warily. "Come in."

He did just that, closing the door carefully behind him. He shoved his left hand in the front pocket of his slacks and leaned against the doorjamb, keeping his distance. He was wearing khakis and an emerald-green polo shirt she'd given him for Christmas the year before. She loved the way he looked in that shirt. The color was one of his best. *She wouldn't be buying him anything for Christmas this year.* The thought caught her by surprise, and caused an unexpected little prickle of pain around her heart.

"I thought I'd better tell you Nana's invited me for dinner tonight," Dean said. "I don't know what she wants to celebrate. I didn't even finish in the top five." The win had gone to Justin Murphy, who now stood in sixth place in the standings.

"You finished high enough to move up in the standings. That's what Nana wants to celebrate, and you know it," she said. "I didn't get a chance to congratulate you yesterday." She had taken a commercial flight back to Charlotte, to avoid their being together on the team plane, and left the race track only minutes after the checkered flag was waved. "Seventeen points between you and the leader. It's the tightest points race since they instituted the Chase."

"Yeah, well, I'd be happier if I was a hundred points up on O'Bryan."

She didn't want to talk about racing. They only fought when they did that. "Of course you have to come out to the farm for dinner. Nana would be upset if you begged off. I'll call and tell them I'm working late here so you can enjoy your evening with them."

He pushed away from the doorframe and stalked across the room to her desk. He wasn't a big man, a couple inches under six feet, broad in the shoulders and narrow in the hips, but intimidating when he put his mind to it. He put both hands on the desktop and scowled down at her.

"I'm not driving you out of our home. I'll make some excuse to Nana and my grandfather."

She sighed. "Don't be ridiculous. It's as much your home as mine. More, really since it's Milo and Nana's house we live in."

"I don't give a rat's ass about whose house it is."

"You're right. There will be other things to argue about in the property settlement."

"We're not going to be arguing about property settlements," he said, his eyes so fierce she felt a little unfamiliar pang of uneasiness.

"No," she said. "We won't. We'll split everything equitably when the time comes. As for tonight I think we can still manage to get through a meal at the same table together without causing a scene."

"I can," he said flatly.

"So can I," she replied sharply. "It's just that, well—" She pushed back her chair and stood up so that she didn't have to stare up into those sexy, dark brown eyes of his. "If we do both show up at the farm tonight Nana will think—"

"That we might be reconciling?" he asked quietly, moving back a step as she came around the corner of her desk. "I doubt she'll think that."

"It's what she wants," Patsy replied. "And she's a very determined woman. She usually ends up achieving what she sets out to do."

"A reconciliation may be what Nana wants for us. But what about you, Patsy?"

"Dean, please. We've been over this and over this."

Was she just being stubborn now? Had she gone so far down her lonely path there was no turning back? Did he even want her back? She dared a look at his face. He looked happier than she had seen him in a long while. But why? Because they were talking, however obliquely, about a reconciliation? Or was it because he was driving so well?

That was probably it. He was within striking distance of what he wanted most in the world. At the moment, she, and their faltering marriage, was more of a distraction than anything else. She tightened her grip on her failing resolve.

He threw up a hand in surrender. "I know. You're not coming back to me. You don't have to say it. I can read it in your body language. Fine. Let's get back to what I came in here to talk about. Steve and Heidi can't make it, but Larry and Crystal are going to try and drop by for coffee and dessert. Kent and Tanya and Sophia will be there."

"Then that settles it. We'll eat as a family," she said, wrapping her arms beneath her chest. A sudden sharp pain had knifed through her heart as it sometimes did, even after all these years when she thought of her children.

All three of them.

"You're thinking of her again, aren't you?" Dean asked. He had come up behind her so softly she hadn't heard him move. She jumped a little in surprise, but didn't shake off his hand when he placed it on her arm.

"Just for a moment," she said, the dark, terrible feeling of loss that had never really gone away threatening to overwhelm her. "It happens sometimes. Don't you still think of her now and then, too?"

"Yes," he said. "I haven't forgotten our Gina."

"Gina," she whispered softly, sadly. "My arms still ache for her."

Her baby, snatched from her hospital crib, taken from them by a stranger and lost forever, though they had searched for her day and night for months.

"Our little girl," he said slipping his arms around her waist, resting his forehead on her shoulder.

"She would be a grown woman now. Thirty on her next birthday." Kent's twin. Sophia's big sister. "We should have told them about her. When we're gone there won't be anyone to remember her at all."

"We can still tell them," Dean said, pulling her back against him. She didn't fight him. She needed his touch, his warmth, to keep the old grief at bay. They were far enough from the windows that the people below couldn't see them. She couldn't deny him or herself the comfort of the embrace. She relaxed against him, let herself take solace in the familiarity of his hard, muscular body against hers.

"When?" she asked, her voice cracking with emotion. "It never seems as if the time is right. Not today because it's so close to the end of the season, so close to Kent and Tanya's wedding. And then the holidays. We don't want to spoil Christmas with such sadness. Will there ever be a right time?"

He gave her a little shake. "Patsy, stop upsetting yourself. We've been over this before. There will be a right time. And soon. Don't worry about it. A few more days or weeks or months won't make any difference, won't change what's past."

She stiffened, drawing away from him. "Here we are back at square one," she said, swiping at a tear that had escaped from the corner of her eye. She saw Dean's face darken, saw him reach out as if to pull her back to him, but she held up a restraining hand, didn't try to keep the bitterness from etching her words. "But this time you're right, damn it. Now just isn't the time."

"SOPHIA, HONEY. You're late. Let me take your coat and join us." Juliana Grosso, Dean's step-grandmother, rose from her place at one end of the long table and hurried across the big room, bracelets jangling on both wrists, to give her Sophia a hug. Juliana was a big-boned and big-hearted woman in her late seventies. She was a wonderful cook who loved to eat her own cooking and it showed in her wide hips and plump face. She had helped Milo raise Dean and his brother Larry when Milo's son, Alfonso, and his wife, Gina, were swept away in a flash flood while on a camping trip in the mountains.

"Come, Sophia." Milo gestured from the other end of the table. Milo and Juliana had been married nearly fifty years. Juliana never tired of telling whomever would listen that no one who knew them back in the day had expected them to stay together any time at all. The difference in their ages alone should have doomed the marriage. Not to mention the fact that Juliana had been a lounge singer in her younger days, the exact opposite in temperament and lifestyle from the widowed FBI agent she'd loved at first sight. "Your food is getting cold, Sophia. Come. Sit. Eat."

Sophia returned Juliana's hug and bent to give her tiny, wizened great-grandfather a kiss on the cheek while Juliana hung her coat on one of the brass hooks by the back door and resumed her place at the end of the long pine table. "I'm sorry, Grandpa. I— Something came up I had to attend to."

"Something at work?" Juliana asked, picking up a casserole dish of lasagna and handing it to Kent to pass to his sister. Kent's fiancée, Tanya, now seated on Sophia's right hand, poured her a glass of wine.

Sophia took a sip. "Mmm, nice. Thanks, Tanya." Dean watched his daughter from across the table. Her shoulders were tensed and he could see the sheen of tears in her blue eyes. Patsy's eyes. Kent had inherited them, too.

He always wondered if Gina's eyes would have been the same intense blue or would she have taken after his side of the family, with dark eyes and hair? He would never know, of course. And with the realization, as it had every time he thought of her over the years, pain seared his heart and his soul.

Patsy was right. Their darling, lost little girl shouldn't be forgotten. But as usual, whenever they had anything to discuss these days, no matter how important to both of them, they had ended up arguing about it.

"A toast," Milo was saying, enjoying his place of honor at the head of the table. "To my grandson. And to my great-grandson for another fine race. May the championship go to the best man. So long as he's a Grosso!"

Everyone raised their glasses and brought them to their lips. Milo sat his glass back down on the table and picked up his fork.

Dean kept his gaze fixed on his daughter. Her cheeks had grown red and her mouth had formed into the same tight line he saw so often on her mother's face these days.

She lifted her glass again. "Wait, Grandpa. I want to make a toast."

"Why?" Milo asked, tucking his head down into his shirt collar as he did whenever he suspected a challenge to his authority, or just someone with enough courage to voice a difference of opinion.

"I want to toast the winner of the race. To Justin Murphy," she said defiantly.

"I don't drink to Murphy wins."

"Milo." Patsy was seated on the old man's left, with an empty chair between her and Dean. She placed her hand on Milo's skinny arm, and cast a beseeching glance at Juliana.

"Why not, Grandpa? He drove a great race. Even Dad said so when they interviewed him on TV last night."

"Liars and cheats the whole lot of them," Milo said

stubbornly, his face set, his eyes defiant. "Worse than that. Louts. Skirt chasers."

"That's enough, Milo," Juliana said quietly. "I will not have such talk at my dinner table."

"That's not true," Sophia said, but her face had turned pale and her lips trembled. "Justin is an honorable man. And I love him. Why can't you accept that?"

"There's bad blood in the boy." Milo wagged his finger at his wife. "Mark my words. He'll come to a bad end like the rest of his clan and break our Sophia's heart."

CHAPTER SEVEN

"FOR THE GUY who just won Phoenix and moved
himself up three places in the standings, you don't look
very happy." They were in Hugo's small, messy office
at Fulcrum Racing. His uncle was standing beside his
scarred metal desk looking through a stack of phone
messages and Justin was sitting on the big, ugly
mahogany credenza that Dixon Rogers had pawned off
on them years before. Justin was driving well and
winning races. He'd made the Chase for the NASCAR
Sprint Cup, if only by the skin of his teeth, but had
moved up in the standings over the last several races.
There had been no more talk of Turn-Rite Tools
dropping their sponsorship of Justin's car the way there
had been in the spring.

"For a crew chief who wasn't on top of the war wagon
when I won the race you're looking pretty pleased with
yourself," Justin replied. Hugo hadn't traveled to the
Phoenix race. Wade Abraham had called the shots for
the team when Hugo opted to stay home and watch over
Sylvie and Kim as they continued to recover from the
shared ordeal of Kim's kidney transplant.

"Sylvie's feeling better," Hugo said. "And Kim's
doing great, too."

"That's swell."

Hugo dropped the stack of sticky notes on his desk and gave Justin a hard look. "It's more than just jet lag. What's wrong? You should be so pumped up after the way you drove yesterday, you shouldn't need sleep for another forty-eight hours."

He was pumped up, or would be, if he weren't so miserable. His car had run like a dream right off the hauler. Since his sister Rachel had taken over as engine builder for the team, he'd finished well in every race that he wasn't knocked out of.

Yesterday had been no exception. Rafael O'Bryan had shredded a tire and finished near the back of the pack. Bart Branch blew an engine on the eighty-second lap and sprayed the track with oil, wadding up a half-dozen cars. Justin had watched that one through his mirror and avoided another pileup twenty-five laps later that had taken three other cars out of the race, leaving him to fight it out with Sophia's brother. He'd held Kent Grosso off for the last eight laps and nosed across the finish line a few thousandths of a second ahead of him, moving himself into sixth place in the standings, while Dean and Rafael O'Bryan were all knotted up in the points lead with one race left to go.

He'd been the one in Victory Lane but Sophia's father's run at the NASCAR Sprint Cup Series championship led all the sports broadcasts.

"I'm happy as hell," Justin said, looking down at his crossed legs, avoiding meeting his uncle's direct gaze.

Hugo snorted. "Yeah, if you were any happier looking you'd be bustin' out cryin'. Anything you want to talk about?"

"I'm glad Kim and Sylvie are coming along so well. I was hoping you'd think she was strong enough to release me from my promise not to tell Sophia the truth about how my dad died."

Hugo shrugged his hands into his pockets and turned to stare out the bank of windows that looked onto a back lot filled with outdated chassis and Dixon Rogers's motor home. "I know I've been asking a lot of you keeping a secret like that from the woman you're going to marry. I'm just not sure Sylvie's strong enough yet for that kind of emotional scene."

"You're still worried about her. I can understand that."

"We came so close to losing both of them." Hugo's voice cracked. He remained with his back to Justin, fighting his emotions.

Justin straightened his shoulders, suddenly as tired as he'd pretended to be earlier. He couldn't pressure his uncle any further. He'd have to go on keeping his secret from Sophia. He just hoped it wouldn't be much longer. "I understand."

"It's not only Sylvie," Hugo said, turning to face his nephew, his expression troubled. "It's Kim, too. She's on so much medicine. She's pushing herself just as hard as Sylvie. Keeping them from overdoing it is like herding cats, let me tell you. Thank God Wade is keeping an eye on Kim. I can focus on Sylvie." He looked harried and Justin felt a twinge of regret. "I'll talk to her, Justin. Soon."

"Sure." He couldn't blame Hugo. He was protecting the woman he loved, keeping a secret that could derail their new life together. *The way his own was heading off the tracks.* He moved to the door. "Is there anything else we need to discuss before the team meeting tomorrow?" he asked, his hand on the doorknob.

Hugo glanced at the clock on the wall. "Nothing that can't wait, I guess. I'll see you in the morning. Seven-thirty. Sharp."

"I'll be here." Justin didn't have to worry about over-sleeping. He'd spent most of the last few nights lying awake, worrying.

Sophia was avoiding him. She hadn't walked him to his car. She hadn't been with him in Victory Lane, and hadn't answered a single call. Something was up and he had a really bad feeling about it.

"I'm heading out now if we're through. I need to find Sophia."

Three hours later he drove by her apartment for something like the tenth time and finally saw her car in its usual spot. He angled his truck into a space in the parking lot and hurried up the walk. He had an idea where she'd been since she got off work. At the farm, Milo and Juliana's place out in the country. Juliana was a great cook and Mondays were her days to cook for the family. Sophia seldom missed a Monday night dinner.

She'd never invited him to attend.

He rang the bell and waited in the small pool of light outside her front door.

He heard her moving around inside the apartment and then the door opened.

"You've been crying," he said, not bothering with any preamble. "What's wrong?"

"Nothing," she said, not very convincingly. Her nose was red and her eyes swollen with tears. He hated to see her cry. It tore him up inside.

Justin took her in his arms. "You're a lousy liar," he said. He didn't need three guesses to know what had caused her tears. She had been at the farm. She had been with her family. Their attachment had caused another argument around the family table.

"Milo again?" he asked and she started crying harder.

"I had another argument with Grandpa."

"Over me?"

"Over us," she said, lifting her face and winding her arms around his neck. "I love you, Justin. I'll always love you but I love Milo, too. And he's old. So old. He might have a stroke and die in his sleep before I can say I'm sorry. I hate that." She sniffed back another tear.

Justin laid his forehead against hers. Sophia teared up easily. He was getting used to her crying, but he still didn't like it. "We'll make it, Sophia. We'll make them come around. All of them. I promised you, didn't I?"

He lifted her chin with the tip of his knuckles and placed his mouth on hers. "I always keep my promises, remember."

PATSY DIDN'T USUALLY drop in on her daughter unannounced, at least not since Justin Murphy had come into her life, but this morning she was worried about her and made the short detour to Sophia's apartment on her way to the garage. She parked at the curb, intending to catch her before she left for work, just to make sure Sophia wasn't still upset about the night before. Milo had been particularly crotchety at dinner and the two had had a sharp exchange of words over Justin Murphy. Sophia had left without having dessert, which upset Juliana. Tanya and Kent weren't immune to the undercurrents swirling around the family table and they didn't stay much longer, Kent pleading an early morning radio interview as an excuse. The atmosphere was so charged even Juliana was relieved when Dean's brother, Larry, called to beg off dessert and coffee for himself and Crystal.

Then it was just the four of them again, as it had been for the last several years since Dean and Patsy had moved into their suite on the second floor of the rambling old farmhouse. Milo had mellowed slightly with the help of one of Juliana's famous highballs and the attention of his grandson. Dean had had two servings of tiramisu and helped Juliana with the dishes, teasing and flattering her until she was flushed with pleasure before sitting down in front of the big-screen TV to watch a documentary on African wildlife with Milo. Having him back with them, even for a short time, did the elderly couple a world of good.

Patsy had bid them all "good night" and climbed the stairs to her room with a raging headache, shutting the heavy oak door tightly to keep the possibility of hearing Dean's low, rumbling laughter coming up the stairs to a minimum.

It had been a long sleepless night.

She got out of the car and started up the brick walkway, knowing in her heart of hearts that she would soon have to start looking for an apartment of her own. Villa Grosso had been Milo and Juliana's home for almost half a century. Her living there, estranged from their grandson, deprived them of his company. She loved the older couple and it wasn't fair to them to put them in the middle of her marital strife. She felt the weight of that decision add itself to her other worries as she reached out to tap the brass knocker on Sophia's front door. Just as she lifted her hand the door opened and Justin came out, shrugging his way into a leather bomber jacket as he walked.

He stopped short, one leg in the apartment, one leg out. "Patsy," he said. "We... I," he corrected, "didn't know Sophia was expecting you this morning."

His hair was damp from the shower and he hadn't shaved. He'd obviously spent the night with Sophia. Patsy felt her color rise a little. Sophia was a grown woman, in love with this man, wanting to marry him, but it was still a tad disconcerting, as her mother, to find him coming out of her baby's apartment after spending the night.

"Good morning, Justin," she said smiling to hide her own slight embarrassment. "I needed to talk to Sophia a moment so I stopped by on my way to the garage."

"She's in the shower. I'll let her know you're here," he said, disappearing back into the apartment, then re-appearing a moment later to open the door wide and invite her inside. "Can I take your jacket?" he asked.

"No, thanks. I'm a little chilly this morning. I'll just leave it on."

"Have a seat." He gestured to the sofa and crossed the small room in two strides. She could hear him tap on the bathroom door. Patsy didn't sit down but walked to the sliders that opened onto Sophia's tiny patio. Her daughter and her next-door neighbor and best friend, Alicia Perez, had planted flowers around and between both the patios and the area was filled with plants, a few still in bloom, although with Thanksgiving almost on them, the weather had turned colder over the past week.

She heard Justin behind her and turned to face him. "She'll be right out," he said, zipping his jacket. "I'd get you a cup of coffee but you probably know your way around this apartment better than I do."

"Thanks, I don't need coffee."

"Okay." He still looked discomfited.

"I really did just stop by on impulse, Justin," she said. "I'm not spying on you and Sophia."

"I didn't think you were, ma'am," he replied, not quite convincingly.

"I'd like it if you'd call me Patsy," she said, suddenly wanting him to know she was on their side in this seemingly insurmountable antagonism between the two families.

"Thank you, but I think I'd better stick to Mrs. Grosso until Sophia and I are married."

"All right," she said. "If that's what you want."

"I want your daughter to be happy," he said, hands shoved in the pockets of his jacket. "But I'm beginning to think that's not possible."

She reached out and touched his hand very lightly. "You love my daughter, don't you?"

"Yes, ma'am. I do."

"Then fight for her."

"I'm doing my best. No one on either side wants to budge. I don't care about myself but I thought y'all loved Sophia more than that." He turned on his heel and left her standing in the middle of Sophia's living room with her mouth open.

"You'll never know how much," Patsy whispered, but she was talking to thin air.

"Do you need something, Mom?" Sophia asked. She was standing in the short hallway that led to her bedroom and the tiny second bedroom she used as a study, wearing a fluffy blue robe—which Patsy recognized as Juliana's gift on her last birthday—with her hair wrapped in a towel. On her feet were a pair of slippers embroidered with Dean's number that they'd found in one of the souvenir trailers outside the Talladega track the year before.

Patsy shook her head. "I just stopped by to see how you were as I just finished telling Justin."

"I'm not a happy camper this morning," Sophia said candidly. "I don't like being at odds with Grandpa, but he won't budge." She sat down on the couch and tugged the belt of her robe more tightly around her waist. "Justin's running out of patience and I'm running out of hope."

"Oh, honey, please. Hang in there a bit longer. The season will be over in less than a week, then we'll have a breather before Champions Week and the holidays. Nana and I will keep working on Milo. He'll come around."

"It makes my stomach ache to think that something might happen to him while we're arguing like this." Her voice wavered slightly and she looked down at her hands still clenched tightly on her belt. "I don't think I can live without Justin in my life but I'm afraid I might have to do just that."

"Oh, baby, don't give up."

Sophia looked up. "I might have to, Mom. I love Justin but I can't imagine my life without all of you in it."

Patsy hurried to the sofa and sat down beside Sophia, longing to take her in her arms. But she didn't. She was afraid if she did she would break down, too. "We'll never be estranged. I'll always be here for you and for Justin, I promise."

Sophia laid her head on her shoulder, something she hadn't done in many years. "Thanks, Mom. But what about Dad? I love him, too. I want him to be happy for me."

"I'll see that your father comes around, also," Patsy said with far more confidence than she felt.

Sophia called her bluff. "How?" she asked, her blue eyes swimming with tears. "How can you make him see past his prejudice against Justin when you can't even solve your own problems? What went wrong between you? Why can't you work through it?"

Patsy stood up, too agitated to remain seated. Part of her wanted nothing more than to open her mouth and tell Sophia all the things that she had bottled up inside her, the grievances, big and small, the heartache, the regrets. But she couldn't do that. Sophia was a grown woman, with heartaches of her own and the understanding that went with them. But she was still her daughter, her baby, her little girl. She couldn't and wouldn't add to her misery. It wasn't fair. To Sophia or to Dean.

"What's come between your father and me is something that is hard to put into words. I guess I'll have to fall back on that horrid cliché about us just having grown apart."

Sophia rose from the couch, too, her expression filled with sadness. "It might be a cliché but it describes exactly what scares me so. If you and Dad have grown apart after all the good years you've had together then what chance do Justin and I have at all?"

CHAPTER EIGHT

DEAN WAS SITTING on top of the pit wall watching the last of the go-or-go-home cars attempt to qualify as the shadows crept across the track, cooling the asphalt, giving them a chance to run a faster lap than the earlier cars, and improve their chances of making the race. He'd been in that position a lot of times his first few seasons driving NASCAR Sprint Cup Series cars. It was hard not to root for the underdogs even now—as long as they didn't better his qualifying time.

Toby Finkler, a long-time driver nearing the end of his career, and a couple years younger than Dean, if you believed his bio, had just made his run, a fast one, for one of the shoestring, single-car teams, about as rare as hen's teeth these days, when a cable TV reporter appeared out of nowhere with his cameraman and his microphone, catching him off guard.

"Hey, Dean. Got a minute for a few questions?"

Dean was too much the professional to get up and walk away even if the last thing he wanted today was to give another interview. "Sure," he said. "Fire away."

"First, congratulations on your driver winning the Nationwide race today. Your Cargill-Grosso truck finished in the top five last night, as well. Do you think the streak will carry over for you in the race tomorrow?"

"Davy Andleman and the BonaFide Replacement Parts team drove a heck of a race this afternoon," Dean said, praising his young driver and automatically including his sponsor's name. "It's been a stressful week for him. His wife's going to have a baby real soon and I know he had a lot on his mind worrying about them, but he never let it affect his driving. He stayed up on the wheel and didn't let himself get psyched out by what was going on around him. The whole BonaFide Replacement Parts team stayed on their game and it showed when the checkered flag came down."

"It was an exciting race," the reporter said with a touch of condescension in his voice that raised the short hairs at the nape of Dean's neck, but he didn't let his irritation show. "But regardless of how your young drivers did this weekend, you still have to finish in the top five or better on Sunday to have any chance of overtaking Rafael O'Bryan for the title. You didn't qualify all that well today. How do you think you'll do tomorrow?"

The reporter pushed the microphone a fraction of an inch closer to Dean's face and waited for him to respond. He wondered what the guy would do if he shoved it right back at him? Probably sue the pants off him. It looked as if he'd had a lot of dental work done to himself. Not to mention the hair implants, and Dean wouldn't have been a bit surprised to find out he was wearing some kind of man-girdle under his knockoff driver's uniform. He didn't look to be the type to spend a couple of hours a day in the gym.

Trouble was the older he got the more nervous he got come qualifying time. Sure he had the hours behind the wheel, the tricks-up-his-sleeve advantage that a quarter century of stock car racing gave him over the younger drivers, but it didn't help. He still got himself wound up tight on qualifying day. He'd just gotten a lot better at hiding the butterflies. Didn't mean the adrenaline wasn't still pumping through his veins making him wish he could act on the impulse to knock the reporter flat on his backside.

"I'm not trying to beat the spread," he drawled after letting the reporter squirm for a minute or two. "I intend to win the race. The conditions out there today weren't optimal for the setup we're using." He shrugged. "We weren't as lucky with the weather as we hoped. We went out first, in the heat of the afternoon without a cloud in sight." He squinted up at the hazy, blue Florida sky, overcast with late-afternoon clouds. "The later guys got the better weather." He put both hands on his knees. It had been a long day and he was tired but he could give this kind of interview in a coma. "That's racing. If I drive good tomorrow, stay in the groove and stay out of trouble we won't be worrying about fifth or better. We'll take it all."

"But you're starting from the back half of the pack. How do you intend to get to the front and stay there?"

Didn't any of these jokers understand stock car racing at all? Some of them did. He suspected this one didn't, but regardless of their knowledge the clock ruled their lives. Dean swallowed his impatience. He framed the hours and days of strategizing and fine-tuning into one short sound bite. "Like I just said, I'm going to do my best to stay out of trouble and drive the wheels off the car."

"Best of luck to you." The reporter's eyes took on a speculative look. "But what about distractions taking you off your game plan? How are you dealing with those?"

"What distractions? The Smoothtone Music team is working like, well, clockwork." He grinned for the camera's benefit but inside he was cold as ice. He knew what the reporter was getting at. He just didn't want to answer.

"What about you and Patsy?" the man persisted. "The rumors are flying about you two. She hasn't been around much these last few races, has she? Are you and your wife headed for a divorce? How's that going to affect your driving tomorrow?"

Dean rose to his feet and even though the other man topped him by six inches he took a quick step back. Dean leaned close and thumped his knuckle on the guy's chest. "I'm going to pretend you never said that," he growled. "And if you ever want another interview from me or any of the other Cargill drivers you'll make sure that section of your tape somehow gets itself wiped clean." He sliced a look at the cameraman, who held up one hand in a gesture that conveyed his intention to stay out of the confrontation. "Got that?"

"Sure. Sure. Don't worry. I won't use it."

"That would be smart. I've got a long memory when it comes to that kind of thing." He turned on his heel and walked toward his pit stall only to find Patsy watching the exchange from the shade of the white tarp the team had erected to keep the Florida sun at bay while they worked.

She was dressed much like the male members of the team in a blue shirt and dark pants, but that's where the resemblance ended. A Cargill Motors sun visor shielded her face. She seldom wore anything with his Smoothtone Music logo on it anymore he realized suddenly, hadn't for a couple of months now. Her opal earrings winked in the sunlight. A tiny gold cross, the one he'd given her after Gina was taken, to remind her to have faith, lay against her throat. Her hair was lighter today. She'd been at the beauty shop again, he guessed. It lay smooth and sleek against her chin and he had a sudden urge to reach out and run his fingers through it, see if it was as soft and silky to the touch as it looked.

"Goodness, what did he say to get you riled up like that?" she asked.

"He asked about you."

"Sorry," she said. "I should have guessed."

"Yeah. They're getting braver about poking around in our private lives these past couple of races. Like a pack of jackals. They smell blood."

"I can deal with what they're nosing around about now," she said. "Our separation's one thing, what I can't deal with is if they start digging into our past."

One reporter, Payton Reese, now working for one of the racing networks and married to Justin Murphy's sister Rachel, had come close when he was researching a series on racing families earlier in the season. It had worried them both, adding to the mounting tensions between them. But Payton, new to NASCAR, had never made the connection between the teenage dirt track driver and his young wife whose infant daughter was stolen from a Nashville, Tennessee, hospital, thirty years earlier. Their tragedy hadn't gained national prominence because it occurred just hours before a horrific airliner crash that killed two hundred people and relegated the sad little story to almost instant oblivion. Perhaps if their private tragedy hadn't been pushed out of the news by the larger one, they could have found Gina. He would never know, another regret that would always be with him.

"I suppose it's to be expected they're snooping into our private lives. NASCAR's showbiz nowadays," Patsy said, interrupting his memories.

"I'm not in showbiz. I just drive a race car," Dean growled, although he knew as well as she did that stock car racing was definitely show business now, as well as big business. "Our private life is our own."

"That's why your schedule's full of photo-ops and meet-and-greets, charity fishing tournaments and golf outings."

"I don't play golf," he reminded her. "That's Kent's venue."

"We've come a long way from those hardscrabble dirt track days," she said, and her eyes grew shadowed and he knew her thoughts paralleled his own.

"Yeah. A long way. No more workin' on cars all night with a pickup pit crew and then strapping in behind the wheel the next afternoon."

"Would you really want to go back to that? Living on a shoestring, hauling the car on a trailer from race track to race track, spending your prize money before you'd even earned it?"

"Sunday money, we called it back then." He grinned sheepishly. "It was good times, though."

She didn't return his smile.

"When did you get in?" he asked because he didn't want her to dwell on the terrible loss they'd experienced in those long-ago, vagabond days.

"Nana, Milo and I got here about two hours ago. We drove out from Miami. Milo won't set foot in a helicopter." Many drivers and owners, and fans for that matter, took advantage of the helicopter drop-off service at Homestead. It saved a lot of time sitting in traffic. "It was hard enough getting him on a plane."

"Are they settled in?"

"Milo's napping. Nana's already conferring with Jesse about tonight's menu—" She broke off what she was going to say.

"Don't worry about the table arrangements. I'll stop by and have a beer with Milo and Nana. Then I'll eat with the guys at the hauler. We've got some simulations to look over."

"That would simplify things." She tilted her head and looked at him from beneath her visor rim. "Have you seen Sophia today?"

"No. It's been crazy around here." A car coming off its practice laps caused him to raise his voice. "I imagine she's with Murphy."

"I hope so," Patsy said. "I'm worried about those two."

"She'd be better off without him." He didn't know why he said that. He really didn't believe it anymore. He'd seen Justin mature over the course of the long NASCAR season. He no longer thought Troy Murphy's son marrying his daughter was the worst thing that could happen to her. He wasn't happy about it but he wouldn't stand in their way.

"Damn it, Dean. You sound just like your grandfather. There's nothing wrong with that boy. He'll make her a fine husband one day."

"Better take it down a notch or two. There are reporters everywhere you look today. It's show business, remember. We're always on," he responded. He'd gotten a rise out of her. He hated the cool, detached way she spoke to him these days. He preferred her anger, at least then he knew he could still evoke some kind of emotion in her if she was spitting mad at him.

She glanced surreptitiously in the direction of the white-tented open-air, hospitality suites perched above the garages. "I won't be drawn into another argument with you, Dean," she said. "Especially not here in front of half the pit crews in the lineup. Not to mention the fans up there in the 'garage suites' staring down at us."

"You brought the subject up."

She puffed out a breath of air, venting a little of her frustration. "You're right. I did. I apologize."

"Look," he said, suddenly weary of sparring with her. He didn't want to fight. He wanted to take her in his arms and hold her close, carry her off to their motor home and make love to her the way they'd made up after all their spats through the years. It was the most bizarre aspect of their whole separation. The woman whose body he'd known intimately for more than half their lives was as off-limits to him as the moon. "I've got to get moving," he said.

"I'll hang around here for a while longer so you can have your time with Nana and Milo."

He dragged his sunglasses off and studied her expression, the fine lines at the corners of her eyes, the laugh lines around her mouth that only made her more lovely in his eyes. "Is this the way it's going to be for us from now on?"

She didn't hesitate as her eyes met his. "Yes," she said, "unless tomorrow is your last race."

CHAPTER NINE

"WHAT ARE YOU DOING back here by yourself?"

"Waiting for my supper," Justin said, swinging his legs down from the black leather banquette in the space at the very back of the Fulcrum Motors hauler that served as the nerve center of the team. The small room housed computer equipment, the built-in benches and table where Justin was sitting that doubled as a conference and dining table, a couple more chairs and an under-counter refrigerator stocked with the bottled water brand that was one of Justin's secondary sponsors.

"Oh," Hugo said, frowning. "I figured you'd be off with Sophia Grosso somewhere celebrating your taking the pole. I saw her go by in a Club Car a few minutes ago. She was heading this way." Outside the sun was setting and the warm Florida autumn afternoon was giving way to evening. Behind Hugo, Justin could hear the team members laughing and joking as they gathered around the huge gas grill where they were fixing the night's meal. They had a right to celebrate. He had won the pole; his first at this track.

"I don't have plans to see Sophia tonight. She's spending the evening with her family. They're all here.

Her uncle Larry and Crystal Hayes. Her cousin and her fiancé. Even Old Milo and Juliana. It's like a Grosso family reunion back in the lot." Justin crossed his arms on the table, doing his best not to sound like he was whining. But that's what he felt like doing. He hadn't had five minutes alone with Sophia since she arrived in Florida the day before. They'd had a few hurried conversations by cell phone, and she'd been at one or two of the social functions that the drivers were more or less required to attend, but there were too many watchful eyes at the public events for them to act like anything other than just friends and acquaintances.

"I noticed they'd pulled in a lot of motor homes. Alan Cargill's here again this week, I hear."

"Why not? His driver's got a chance to win it all."

"And he's probably doing damage control on the buyout," Hugo speculated. "I hear he's brought his boy, Nathan, in from Boston to help with the deal-making."

Justin lifted one shoulder in a shrug. "I wouldn't know."

Hugo altered the subject. "With Alan Cargill showing up it's like the royal family of NASCAR's all here."

"Yeah, something like that."

"And when the royal family's gathered there's no place for a jumped-up Murphy courtin' the princess."

"C'mon, Hugo. Don't gloat. You're getting what you wanted. Sophia and I are barely communicating. I thought by now we'd have set our wedding date. Instead, I'm sneaking around trying to find a few minutes alone with her just like I was eight months ago." Justin reached into the little refrigerator and pulled out a bottle of water, removing the lid with one violent twist.

Hugo dropped heavily into a chair, pushed away from the computer counter, put his hands on his knees and looked down at the floor. "You've got it all wrong about me not wanting you and Sophia to be happy, Justin. Hell, how can I be that selfish when I've found Sylvie again after all these years?"

"You know I'm glad for the two of you but it doesn't help me and Sophia."

"Hang on, Justin," Hugo said, as near to pleading as Justin had ever heard his uncle get. "It won't be much longer, I swear. As soon as I think Sylvie is strong enough to handle it we'll get the word out that Dean Grosso, or any of them, had nothing to do with Troy's death."

"But what about Connor? You still think old Milo, or someone answering to him, ran him off that mountain all those years ago, don't you?"

"What does it matter what I think about it?"

"'Cause those damned Grossos are stubborn as hell. They won't forgive or forget." He didn't add *just like you*. He didn't have to. "When you get right down to it, Sophia and I are still caught between a rock and a hard place."

"Justin? Hugo? Are you back here?"

It was Rachel's voice calling from the narrow hallway that bisected the hauler. The door opened and she stepped inside the conference room. At the sight of her excited, happy face Justin couldn't bring himself to argue any more with their uncle. "What's up, Rayray?" he asked.

"Supper's ready," she said, laughing, glowing really, like he'd always heard happened to pregnant women. He couldn't help but grin inside. He was going to be an uncle before too much longer. Didn't that beat all. "Come and get it. Grilled chicken breast, cheeseburgers, steamed veggies and loaded baked potatoes. If you don't get a move on the guys will finish it off before we even get a chance to eat."

"On our way, Rachel," Hugo said, giving Justin a look that seemed to ask for his patience and his forgiveness at the same time.

Justin looked at his sister's face. She wasn't troubled by the mysterious deaths in their family's past. Why should she be? Her happiness didn't depend on it. She had come into her own this season. She had taken over the engine building for the team when Johnny Melton had let his personal problems get the best of him. Her expertise and hard work had enabled Justin to drive himself out of the hole Melton's subpar engines had dropped him into. She had fallen in love and married Payton Reese, a hell of a guy, in Justin's opinion. She was going to have a baby in the new year. Right now the world was Rachel's oyster and he wasn't about to go crying on her shoulder.

"You kids go ahead. I need to make a phone call," Hugo said, turning to face them, his emotions under control once more. "I want to check on Sylvie. Make sure she's not overdoing it while I'm away. I wish Sylvie and Kim had come, but the doctor wanted them both to rest a bit more so they'll watch the race on TV."

"Tell Sylvie we said 'hi,'" Rachel said. "And try not to be too long."

"Save me a cheeseburger with the works."

"I'll do my best. I need to get some food for Payton, too. He's on his way from an interview with Alan Cargill about selling Cargill Racing to Dean and Patsy Grosso." She made a little face. "Will you have a few minutes to give him your thoughts on the race and the Chase, little brother?"

"Not if you call me that again."

"Please, Justin Murphy, greatest NASCAR driver of his generation?"

"That's better. Sure I've got a few minutes for Payton. I've got nothing else planned for the evening."

She looked from him to Hugo and back again. She tilted her head, her expression quizzical. "Everything okay back here? I thought you were just in here gloating that you beat out everyone." She gave him a little punch on the shoulder. "Pole sitter. Sounds good, doesn't it?"

"Sounds fantastic, engine builder," Justin said, urging her out into the corridor. "I'm starving and we need to celebrate with our team."

"Next year we will be the best. You will be NASCAR Sprint Cup Series champion. Mark my words."

"It's a deal," he said, pushing the residue of the unsettling conversation with Hugo out of his thoughts. If there was one thing you learned early on driving a race car, it was to concentrate on the here and now and let everything else take care of itself.

The atmosphere under the raised tailgate at the back of the mammoth hauler, which was parked with laser precision alongside forty-two others in the race track's infield, was upbeat and jovial. The south Florida sunset was a huge wash of orange and purple and gold, a perfect backdrop to the yellow and turquoise grandstand rising out of the flat Florida landscape. Charcoal smoke and the smell of grilling meat drifted between the haulers and beautiful women in tight tops and tighter jeans strolled by often enough to make keeping an eye out for them worthwhile. Justin worked hard to enjoy himself as much as the others, but a part of him was always on the lookout for Sophia, hoping he'd catch a glimpse of her at either her brother's or her father's hauler, or just walking by, enjoying the warm Florida night.

He spent fifteen minutes with Payton Reese while he ate, partly to satisfy Rachel but mostly because he liked his brother-in-law and knew his interview would be a fair one. He finished his cheeseburger, had a second beer and then said his good-nights. He grabbed one of the team's golf carts and wended his way back to the motor home lot, waving to friends, trading quips with fans, never quite slowing down enough to get caught up by autograph hunters. Then he spotted her, moving away from him through one of the smaller gates leading to the fan pavilion.

He was wearing jeans and a Daytona t-shirt, a souvenir from his first race there four years ago, a Turn-Rite ball cap and his trademark wraparound sunglasses. He stuck the sunglasses in his back pocket, turned the ball cap around, tucked the lanyard with his hard pass inside his shirt and sauntered past the guard at the gate with a wink and a nod.

"Good luck." The guard waved back. "I'm not wadin'

into a crowd to save you if they recognize you," he warned.

"They won't," Justin said. He'd tried this gambit before and it had worked every time.

Thirty seconds later he caught up with Sophia outside a tent selling die-cast replicas of NASCAR Sprint Series Cup cars and other race track souvenirs.

"Hi there, pretty lady," he drawled in his best *Dukes of Hazzard* imitation, hands shoved in his pockets as he perused the models on sale looking for one of his own No. 448 car. "Could I buy y'all a drink?"

Sophia glanced at him from the corner of her eye, taking a step sideways as she did so. "No, thank you—" Her tone was polite but chilly. Then she recognized him. "Justin? What are you doing out here?" She hissed. She looked around. "No one's with you? You'll be mobbed if you're recognized."

"Nah," he said, spotting a No. 448 car model in the reverse paint scheme he'd run at Talladega the year before. He didn't have one like it. He picked it up and reached into his pocket. "Damn," he said. "I forgot my billfold."

"I can hold it for you, Justin," the heavyset, middle-aged man behind the counter said just a little too loudly not to be overheard by the half-dozen other people inspecting his wares. "I'd let you take it with you now, but I'd lose my job if I did that."

Recognition rippled through the shoppers and began spreading through the crowd ambling among the blue-and-white tents and groupings of potted flowers and towering palm trees. People began to stop and stare, nudging their companions, inching closer.

"Oh, good grief, now look what you've done." Sophia pulled out a trio of bills and almost threw them at the dealer. "Here. That should cover it. Get your car, Justin. If we don't get moving you'll be stuck here signing autographs until they close the place down."

"Yeah," he said, slightly surprised by how quickly he'd been recognized. Making the Chase for the NASCAR Sprint Cup, even at the tail end of it, had certainly raised his recognition factor. Diane, his Motor Media Group PR rep, would be proud of him.

"Let's go." Model in one hand, Sophia's hand in the other, he slipped into the crowd with her and they quickly made their way back to the gate. Luck was on their side. At almost the same moment Justin had been recognized by the model dealer the public address speaker announced the start of a free concert by a well-known local rock band sponsored by a soft drink company. The sudden surge of race fans toward the stage set up at the end of the fan zone helped cover their retreat.

"Told you you'd get in trouble out there," the guard said with a grin, waving them through. "Better hightail it on back to the drivers' and owners' lot before they spot you in here, too."

"The drivers' lot's not such a good idea, either," Justin muttered as he climbed into the golf cart beside Sophia and headed back into the infield of the race track.

"Why not?" Sophia asked. "At least no one there's going to be hounding you for an autograph."

Justin snorted. "That's for sure. The Grossos have got what? Four motor homes lined up there like the front line of a football team? All of them with a water view and their backsides pointed in my direction." During NASCAR events the drivers' motor homes were parked around the largest of two man-made lakes.

"If you want to get technical there's five counting Alan's unit," Sophia said, smiling. It had been a long while since he'd seen her so carefree. "Okay, you made your point. Where do you suggest we go to be alone?"

It had grown dark while they wandered through the fan zone. The moon had risen and was shining down on the infield, quiet at this time of day. "How about a moonlight stroll along the lakeshore?"

"We won't be alone there, either. And besides you never know if an alligator might pop out at you." She shivered. "Ugh." The race track was built on the edge of the Everglades and wildlife, including the occasional alligator, sometimes breached the perimeter fence and made it onto the grounds, if not the track itself.

"Yeah, you're right there. But it's damned near as hard to keep your mind on the moonlight and stardust knowing your great-grandfather's sitting in his lawn chair with a shotgun across his knees waiting to take a potshot at me."

"Shame on you. Grandpa would never do that." Sophia punched him on the shoulder hard enough to make him yelp. The cart swerved a little and she tumbled against him. He took the opportunity to put his arm around her and keep her close.

They veered away from the lake and headed toward the garages. Hospitality suites topped the low building with a serrated edging of white cabana-style tents, a feature of the Florida track that gave fans a unique opportunity to catch the action in the pits and the garages at the same time. The garages were quiet now, closed and locked for the night. No one would be allowed inside until the morning. Pit road was also quiet, a far cry from what it would look like in eighteen hours.

"Want to hang out and enjoy the moonlight?" he asked, wondering if they could somehow sneak into one of the garage suites, deciding it probably wasn't possible. The race track's security was some of the best he'd seen on the circuit.

Sophia laid her hand on his arm. "Not tonight, Justin. I think I should get back to Grandpa and Nana. They'll be turning in early. I want to say good-night."

He rested both arms on the small steering wheel. "Will you come to my trailer after they go to bed?"

"No," she said. "I don't think I should."

She kept her face averted. He studied her profile, the now familiar rush of anxiety at the thought of losing her made his palms sweat. "I miss you so damned much, Sophia. We haven't been alone together for days. It's almost as if you're avoiding me. Is that it, Sophia? Are you having second thoughts?"

She turned to face him then, her expression somber, her eyes darkened with the same anxiety he was feeling. "Second and third thoughts," she admitted, reaching out to touch his cheek. "I want a family. I want a marriage that will last like Grandpa's and Nana's." He noticed she didn't mention her parents and he felt her pain. "I want to still be married when we're old and gray and set in our ways. I'm worried we might not have the strength to bring that off."

"We love each other," he said, wanting to take her in his arms but holding back. The track was quiet but it wasn't deserted. The last thing he wanted was for some camera-toting fan or reporter with a long lens to peer through the fence and catch them in an embrace that would be plastered all over the Internet before morning. "We'll make it work." Then he ignored his own advice and reached out to take her in his arms.

Their lips met and he shifted on the narrow seat to better fit her to him. She wrapped her arms around his neck, pressed against him and let her mouth open beneath the pressure of his. The kiss went on and on. She began to relax against him, began to return the kiss, held his face between her hands and demanded another when the first one ended.

"I love you, Justin. When I'm with you I can believe anything's possible."

"Then come back to the Manor with me after you say good-night to Milo and Juliana. Stay with me. Make love to me."

She rested her forehead against his. "I can't," she whispered. "Even though I want to more than anything. I'm sorry, Justin." He could hear the tears in his voice, knew they would be sparkling in her blue eyes.

He sighed. Arguing with her would only upset her more. "I won't bully you, Sophia. I won't make you choose between me and your family. Not tonight. I'm not that selfish. Tomorrow is the biggest day of your dad's career."

She caressed his face with the tips of her fingers and kissed him again, sweetly, softly. "You're a good man, Justin. Don't ever let yourself believe you're not. I know you worry that you might someday start behaving the way your father did, but I don't."

"Genetics——" he began. She didn't know all the terrible things he knew about Troy Murphy now. She couldn't begin to guess.

She touched her fingers to his lips. "Blood doesn't always tell. You aren't your father. You weren't raised by him, or shaped by the same forces. And even though Hugo was his brother he turned out fine. So blood doesn't always tell. I love you, Justin. I'll always love you and some day we'll be together despite everything."

He felt an iron band inside him twist and break and begin to melt away. She loved him. She believed in him. He wouldn't fail her. He was not Troy Murphy, a man shaped by circumstances he could never understand. He had some of Troy's characteristics, but not all of them. He had a hell of a temper but it never got the best of him. He didn't bully weaker men or terrorize women. He wasn't perfect but he would try to be for Sophia's sake. "I want to spend every day of the rest of my life with you, Sophia. Is that enough of a pledge?"

"It's more than enough," she said forcefully. "It's all I need to know."

"C'mon, then," he said putting the golf cart into gear. "It's time I get you back to the Grosso fortress, princess. I need to try and get some sleep, although how I'm going to manage that without you beside me, I have no idea."

She curled her arms around his waist and laid her head on his shoulder as he turned the cart and headed back to the conclave of motor homes parked on the lakeshore. In only a minute or two they were there. Reluctantly she moved out of his arms. "Justin, about tomorrow?" He saw the happiness fading from her eyes, replaced once more by a slight uncertainty.

He didn't have to be a mind reader to know what was bothering her now. "Don't worry, Sophia," he said. Drawing on the newfound confidence her declaration had given him, he brushed his knuckles lightly over the soft skin of her jaw. "After you walk me to my car tomorrow you can head over to the Cargill pits and root for your dad with all your heart and soul."

CHAPTER TEN

RACE DAY.

Patsy always woke with butterflies in her stomach and they never went away until the checkered flag dropped, and not always then.

What would she be doing today when the race ended? Would she be with her husband or still alone? Would Dean win the NASCAR Sprint Cup Series championship or be disappointed in his quest yet again? She had never felt so torn. If he won she might possibly prevail in her efforts to get him to retire from stock car racing.

If he lost he would keep coming back again and again until he captured the title, and if he won, he'd want to defend the title. Either way she would be forced to keep her promise and divorce him.

"Good morning," Juliana sang out from the kitchen as Patsy opened the pocket doors that separated the small "guest room" of the motor home from the main living area. "How did you sleep?" The older woman was spooning coffee into the stainless-steel coffee-maker as she talked. Milo was nowhere to be seen but Patsy doubted he was still asleep in the master bedroom. He was always up with the sun.

"Pretty well, I guess," Patsy responded. "I never heard you or Milo get up."

"Milo was up before the chickens. He's off having coffee with the team at the hauler. He'll be back in an hour or so. Why don't you go ahead and take your turn in the bathroom while I finish up here."

"Sounds like a plan," Patsy said, running her fingers through her hair. "Mmm, whatever you're cooking smells delish."

"It's a crustless quiche recipe I clipped out of a magazine. I've been wanting to try it. Loaded with butter and cheese, but it's a special day."

"And a long one," Patsy added.

"Even more reason to keep up our strength. Now scoot. You know it takes an old woman like me a long time to put her game face on." Patsy waved her hand to disavow Juliana's description of herself and kept on smiling all the way into the shower.

When she emerged from her little bedroom twenty minutes later her son and daughter-in-law-to-be were sitting around the built-in banquette drinking coffee and eating cinnamon rolls.

"Oh, Lordy, are those Jesse's cinnamon rolls?" she asked, swirling the tip of her finger through the frosting dripping onto Kent's plate.

"Yes, ma'am. He baked a double batch of them before he left for the beach."

"He knew he couldn't compete with me on a daily basis," Juliana said as she headed for the back of the motor home. "So he took off for a condo in the Keys. Save one of those for me. I'll be out in a jiffy."

"Where's Milo?" Kent asked, tearing off a bite of

cinnamon roll and putting it in his mouth with a sigh of bliss.

"Nana said he's having coffee with the team at the hauler."

"We hoped to be here in time to have breakfast with him," Tanya said, before taking a bite of her own cinnamon roll.

"I should head over there, do a walk-though with him." Kent accepted a refill of his coffee mug with a smile of thanks. "I've got a few minutes before I have to be at the Vittle Farms hospitality tent."

On race weekends most sponsors hosted hospitality suites or tents, stocked with soft drinks and bottled water, big-screen TVs and other amenities, for employees and clients. Sometimes they even served breakfast or lunch. That's where Dean was this morning, Patsy knew. One of the perks of these corporate events was an appearance by the sponsor's drivers. Patsy had always thought it was rather strange that NASCAR was the only major sport that expected its athletes to give pep talks to the fans before the big game. But that was the way it was and probably always would be.

"Milo will like that." Patsy gestured toward Tanya with the coffeepot. Tanya gave her head a shake.

"Thanks, no more for me."

The door of the motor home opened and Sophia appeared dressed for a day in the pits in a long-sleeved mint-green shirt with the sleeves rolled to just below her elbows, tailored slacks and closed-toe shoes. Her hard card dangled from a lanyard around her neck. Sunglasses were pushed up on the top of her head. She was carrying a bag that Patsy guessed contained field glasses and a water bottle and sunblock, a lipstick and hairbrush, probably, her cell phone and a digital camera. At least that's what Patsy always carried in her own shoulder bag.

Sophia eyed the cinnamon rolls on the table. "Oh, good, there are some left. I was afraid you'd eaten them all already."

"Would I do that to you? My favorite sister?"

"Your only sister, might I remind you. Mom, are you okay?" Sophia rushed to get a towel to wipe up the coffee that Patsy spilled when she set her mug down too hard on the table.

"I'm fine. Just fine. How clumsy of me. Tanya, did any of it splash on you? Did you get burned?" How stupid of her to let such a casual remark upset her after all these years. Why was it happening to her now? Because she and Dean had spoken of their lost child, however briefly, and brought the old heartache to the forefront of her thoughts again?

"Not a drop on me," Tanya assured Patsy, but it was easy to read the concern in her eyes.

"Patsy," Juliana sang out from the bedroom. "Will you check the quiche for me? We don't want it overdone."

"Right away," she said.

"I'll get it, Mom," Sophia offered.

"Don't bother. I know right where everything is." Patsy jumped up from her seat, relieved to have the focus of attention switch from her clumsiness to the food.

Juliana pushed open the dividing doors and sailed back into the kitchen. She was dressed in a long denim skirt and a rose-colored tunic. Her silver-gray hair was pulled up in her trademark French twist and a trio of gold and copper bracelets adorned each wrist. She gave the quiche a quick inspection and pronounced it ready to eat.

"Are you going to the prayer service after the drivers' meeting?" Kent asked as Patsy cut the rich egg-and-cheese casserole into serving-size pieces.

"Why do you ask?"

"You always attend with Dad—" He broke off awkwardly. "Sorry, I shouldn't have brought it up."

"I'll be there, Kent. There will be too many reporters hanging around not to have it remarked on if I don't show up." She set a plate in front of him. She laid her hand on his shoulder. "I know my part. I'm the mother of the reigning NASCAR Sprint Cup Series champion, at least for the next ten hours or so, and damned proud of it. I'm the wife of one of this year's contenders and best-loved drivers racing. I'll say all the right things, hit all my marks."

Kent covered her hand with his own. "I know you will, Mom. You're as much of a pro at this business as Dad and I are."

"I'm taking notes," Tanya said.

"Me, too," Sophia said, laying her hand on top of Kent's. "You make it look easy, Mom. You're always so calm, always got it together. You never let them see you sweat."

"Or cry," Juliana said. "That's important, too."

"Amen." Patsy squeezed Tanya's hand and gave Sophia a quick hug. "Let's eat. I'm starved."

Tanya rose from her seat, taking the napkins and silverware that Sophia handed her, setting the table while Sophia took a pitcher of orange juice from the refrigerator and Juliana garnished a glass bowl of fruit with fresh mint. "This is what I like about the Florida races," she said, bringing the dish to the table. "Jesse is always able to buy such lovely fruit. And last night the fish was wonderful. I wish you—and Justin—could have joined us."

Sophia laid her hand on Juliana's arm. "I wish we could have, too, Nana. Someday. Someday soon."

"Of course," Juliana said bracingly. "Now here, let me give you some of this quiche. I'm anxious to know how you like it. I think it would be a great holiday brunch recipe. And Heaven knows they're almost on us already and I have all my shopping to do."

"I'm doing mine on the Internet this year," Sophia said.

"Not me. I intend to set Fifth Avenue on fire during Champions Week. What else is there to do when the guys are flitting from one TV studio to the next giving interviews?" Tanya observed wryly.

"I have never flitted anywhere in my life," Kent insisted between bites of quiche.

"Sorry," Tanya said with a laugh. "I didn't mean to insult your masculinity."

"I've got feelings, too." He grinned back.

"I thought real men didn't eat quiche?"

"When it tastes like this, they do. And ask for seconds." He held out his plate. "Just another bite. Then I'm off to find Milo."

Patsy felt a squeeze of pain somewhere in the region of her heart. She and Dean used to banter back and forth that way. Not for a long time now. Probably never again. She glanced over at Sophia and saw that she was looking down at her plate, making a show of eating but barely touching her food. Her daughter was putting a brave face on the family's continued resistance to her engagement to Justin Murphy, but Patsy knew the stress of it was wearing her down.

One more race, she told herself, digging into her casserole so that Juliana wouldn't be offended. One more race and the season would be over and she could go home and try to sort out the mess her life was in.

CHAPTER ELEVEN

DEAN MOVED restlessly on his chair. He and Kent and Patsy were in the huge tent that served as the track's media center during NASCAR races. They were crammed behind a table, a NASCAR banner behind them, a row of microphones in front of them and a gaggle of reporters, soundmen and cameramen crowding in from the other side of the table. He hated these media grillings, especially on race day. It seemed the older he got the less patience he had for the hoopla surrounding the race. He hadn't realized how much he'd depended on Patsy to keep him grounded as the tension wound him tighter and tighter, until she'd left him.

"Patsy, as one of the most visible women owners in NASCAR, how does it feel?"

How many times had she been asked a variation of that question? Hundreds, he supposed. Before they had bought a truck in the NASCAR Craftsman Truck Series and cars in the NASCAR Nationwide Series, most interviewers had limited themselves to asking her the formulaic questions they asked all the other wives. *How did she feel about having a husband and a son both racing? Who did she root for? What did she say to them before and after a race?*

These days the queries were more along the lines of how hard did she find it to be taken seriously? "I don't find it particularly hard," she'd say softly, leaning forward just a little, flirting with the camera. "Cargill-Grosso Racing doesn't hire employees that aren't smart enough to recognize the person who signs their paychecks is the one they'd better be paying attention to."

Then she would laugh and go on to praise the team and all the hard work they did. She never forgot to stroke the sponsors who backed a team with a woman CEO, and she never failed to give Alan Cargill credit for giving them the chance to get Cargill-Grosso Racing off the ground.

"Patsy, we haven't seen you around as much the second half of the season. Is there a reason for that?" The reporter, a woman, shot a sideways glance at Dean. Under the table he curled one hand into a fist but otherwise didn't let anything show on his face.

"I'm around," Patsy replied, just a bit sharply. "I work twelve-hour days. I do whatever needs to be done. It limits my time to spend at press conferences like this one. That's where a partnership comes in. I run the garage. Dean deals with the media." She had herself under control again, her smile back in place.

"And on top of everything else she accomplishes, she's almost as good a cook as my great-grandmother," Kent joked, leaning forward to give her a grin. "In our family that's the highest compliment you can pay a person."

"With both my husband and my son in the thick of the Chase most of you guys haven't been clamoring for my input," she reminded the assembled pack of media vultures. "And since this is the last chance y'all will have to talk to the two of them before the race starts I suggest you make the most of the opportunity. Thanks, all. Please excuse me. I have to get down to pit road."

She stood up, waving away one last question on who she was rooting for with a laughing "Oh, no, you don't." She leaned down to give Dean a peck on the cheek and Kent a big hug. "I'll see you both at your cars," she said, and walked out of the media center.

Dean watched her disappear through the door. His skin burned where her lips had brushed against his cheek and it took a real effort not to reach up and touch the spot. Her lips had been cool, the kiss without heat, without passion, but even that brief contact had him physically aroused. He didn't know how much longer he could take having her so close by and yet so distant. It was driving him crazy, taking his mind off the race.

Was that what she wanted?

If he lost did she think he would give up and agree to her demand that he retire? Could he walk away from racing if he didn't win the prize he'd coveted for so many years? And, if he did win, the temptation to come back and defend his hard won title would be equally as strong. One choice would lose him his wife. The other his self-respect.

"Dean, are you fully recovered from the crash in the Nationwide race at Phoenix last week? Do you think it will affect your driving today?"

He pulled himself together and singled out the young wire service reporter who had asked the question. "I've had a whole week to rest up. What do you think?" His PR rep, Jane Ratcliff, took her cue and moved to the table.

"Thank you, all of you, for coming. Both Dean and Kent need to be heading to their garages. The opening ceremonies are almost ready to start."

"Can we get a picture of you two together?" someone asked. "A 'may the best man win' money shot?"

"Sure," Kent said. He moved to Dean's side and put his arm around his shoulders. "If I can't repeat as NASCAR Sprint Cup Series champion, then I can't think of a better man to take the title than my dad." He reached out and offered Dean his hand. Dean shook it and then pulled Kent into a bear hug.

"If I can't stay out ahead of O'Bryan today then I sure as hell will be your drafting partner."

"It's a deal." Kent laughed. "But don't do me any favors. Look out for yourself. If today's my day I'll win it on my own."

"Good luck, son."

"Good luck, Dad."

They posed for a few more pictures before their Motor Media Group PR reps hustled them out of the room and into golf carts headed for the driver introduction ceremony. Like being late for, or missing, the drivers' meeting earlier in the day, failure to show up for the driver introductions could jeopardize his starting position. MMG wasn't about to let that happen.

An hour later Dean was back on pit road, his team assembled around him, the videographers with their massive shoulder-held cameras circling around them looking for the best shot, the best angle. Dean held his helmet under his arm and tried not to be too obvious as he searched the crowd for Patsy. Surely she could put aside their differences long enough to walk him to his car?

She hadn't been there at Phoenix last week but she had still been angry. She hadn't seemed that way at the press conference, but then, what the heck did he know. He couldn't read her thoughts, or even pick up on her emotions. She wasn't his Patsy-girl anymore. And if he didn't figure out some way to turn things around between them she never would be again.

"JUSTIN, YOU'RE CLEAR to pass Shakey. He knows you're coming up behind him." The voice of Dennis Murphy, Justin's cousin and spotter, was loud in his earphones.

"Got ya," Justin radioed back. His teammate Ron "Shakey" Paulson had been running strong all day but he was out of the Chase for the NASCAR Sprint Cup. He was a great guy, an old-school driver who was a real team player. He pulled up on the high side as Justin came up on his rear bumper and let him pass. Justin gave him a wave as he roared by and headed on to his next quarry, Rafael O'Bryan.

Justin was running seventh and so far had stayed out of trouble. The three caution flags that had been waved had been for single-car incidents, one for debris on the track. So far, they'd avoided any pileups. The track was clean and he'd found his groove.

The first third of the race had been a battle between Rafael O'Bryan and Kent Grosso with most of the others laying back, watching the two frontrunners duke it out. Will Branch ran out of gas on lap 112, one of those embarrassing mistakes that should never happen to a professional race car driver but too often did, causing the fourth caution of the day. Then on lap 200 the fifth caution of the day came out when one of the go-or-go-home cars blew an engine and sprayed the track with oil, gathering up another couple of lapped cars and thinning the field. Twenty-five laps later Hart Hampton shredded a tire and went into the wall, ending his outside chance at the NASCAR Sprint Cup Series championship.

Justin knew he couldn't win the championship but he could win the race and he was determined to do that if it was humanly possible. He had a fast car, thanks to Rachel. She was one hell of an engine builder. He had a first-rate team, led by Hugo, and a pit crew that was at the top of their form. There was no reason he couldn't be the one in Victory Lane after the checkered flag dropped.

If he did win the race he could finish as high as third in the standings. Then the Grossos would have to stop looking down their noses and take notice of him. Old Milo would have to give him and Sophia his blessing. Especially once the truth about his father's death was finally out in the open between the two families.

He could see Dean Grosso's No. 414 Smoothtone Music car just ahead of him. Sophia's father had worked his way steadily up the grid, stayed cool, drove his way around the trouble spots, and now he seemed to be making his move.

Maybe the veteran driver would pull a miracle out of thin air and win the NASCAR Sprint Cup Series championship? Stranger things had happened. Sophia's father could take it all if Rafael O'Bryan finished out of the money and Dean won the race. Long odds, but stock car racing was as much luck as skill.

FIFTY-ONE LAPS to go. Patsy sat on top of the huge rolling toolbox and jiggled her pen between her fingers. Dean was driving his usual steady, workmanlike race. Sometimes that annoyed her. Sometimes she wanted him to stand on the gas, get up on the wheel and show those youngsters what a real driver could do. But she'd long ago realized that was not his style, not the way he worked. Sure, he'd never won the NASCAR Sprint Cup Series championship but how many other drivers had finished so high in the standings so many years in a row?

That didn't make it any easier for him to accept never having captured that elusive prize, though. Especially after Kent had won the championship the year before. Time was passing Dean by. He had to win soon or end his career the way his grandfather had, without that one last trophy to make it all worthwhile.

That was one of the things that hurt her most, she admitted as she automatically clocked Dean's lap times and kept an eye on Kent's, as well. That she, that their marriage, their partnership, the time they would have to spend together without him flying off all over the country for sponsor commitments and charity appearances, was not enough compensation for not achieving his ultimate goal.

"Mom!" Sophia was pointing at a monitor. "There's a wreck on the back straightaway. Five. Seven. No eight cars!" Her daughter was beside her on the box today, Milo having opted to watch the race from Kent's pit stall. Juliana, as usual, had stayed behind in the air-conditioned comfort of the motor home, watching the network television broadcast and monitoring a closed-circuit feed that the race track provided for drivers and their families.

Patsy stood up but from where they were situated it was impossible to see what was happening. The team, their view equally limited, was glued to the TV screen, as well.

Patsy lifted her hand to her headphones, listening closely. "Go low. Go low," came a tinny, growling voice. It belonged to Roy-Bob Germann, Dean's spotter for the last ten years. "There's two cars tied up in front of you. Stay straight. Stay straight. Whooee! You're through. You're clear."

"Hell of a job, Roy-Bob. Hell of a job." Dean sounded as calm and controlled as he always did on the radio.

"Good driving, man. Real good driving. We just bought ourselves a ticket to the show."

Patsy's heart rate ratcheted higher. Roy-Bob was right, she realized as the cars involved in the wreck began to make their way onto pit road and back to the garage. Two of the Chase for the NASCAR Sprint Cup contenders were being towed. They were out of the race and out of the running.

Kent, in the Vittle Farms car, emerged from the cloud of smoke with Justin Murphy right behind him. Patsy reached out and gave Sophia's hand a squeeze when she identified the orange-and-brown Turn-Rite Tools car.

"They made it! All three of them!" Sophia cried, clapping her hands as the undamaged cars continued to orbit the track under the yellow flag while the debris from the pileup was cleared away. But when it was all sorted out the leader board hadn't changed. Rafael O'Bryan was still on top with less than sixty laps to go.

Patsy waited impatiently for the track to be cleared, Sophia, equally impatient beside her. When the pace car finally veered off onto pit road and the line of race cars behind it accelerated into the straightaway they both surged to their feet unable to remain seated a moment longer. Dean was only inches from O'Bryan's back bumper when the green flag fell.

Five laps later Dean's crew chief passed Patsy a note. "What does it say, Mom?" Sophia asked through her earphones, still having to almost yell.

The note was short and to the point. "If your father passes O'Bryan he'll win the race but lose the championship." The cars roared past with a blast of wind and noise that hit like a physical blow. Patsy took a deep breath and continued. "O'Bryan has to finish farther back than third place."

"Or Dad ends the season first loser," Sophia finished for her. "Kent can't help. He's too far back. It'll take him too long to work his way back up the grid." Kent had gotten bottled up behind a trio of lapped cars and lost eleven spots before he could work his way through the snarl of traffic. It was likely now, that he would not repeat his championship. Patsy felt disappointment wash over her when she realized that, but it didn't last long. Kent had a long career ahead of him. There would be other championships in her son's future, she was certain of it.

"One step at a time," Patsy cautioned. "Let's get

him into the lead first and then worry about finding a
white knight."

"Okay," Sophia said, crossing her fingers. "First
things first." She turned her attention back to the track,
but she couldn't sit still and neither could Patsy. She
remained standing watching the laps come and go.
Watching the race and the season come down to the
wire. Wondering where her faltering marriage would
stand when the checkered flag came down.

CHAPTER TWELVE

"TEN LAPS. TEN LAPS. You're okay on gas. Okay on tires." The voice in his earphones this time was his crew chief, Perry Noble. Nothing fazed Perry. He sounded as though he was asking Dean if he wanted milk in his coffee, not planning strategy to win the NASCAR Sprint Cup Series championship. "Make your move on O'Bryan anytime you're ready."

"I've been ready for the last twenty laps," Dean replied, mindful as always that his voice could be heard by thousands of fans and millions of TV viewers as well as by his team. *Hell, I've been ready for the last twenty years.* The trouble was O'Bryan wasn't cooperating. He wanted this race as much as Dean. He couldn't want it more though, and that was going to be the difference.

Two cars were glued to his back bumper as tightly as he was following the former champion. Two of Dixon Rogers's cars, Shakey Paulson and Justin Murphy. And behind them both was Kent.

Somehow he'd made it back to the front, Dean realized. He had been too busy looking for an opening to make his run at O'Bryan to have paid attention to what was happening in the middle of the pack, but it was good seeing the Vittle Farms car in his mirror again.

"Nine laps," Roy-Bob reminded him. "Anytime, buddy."

He knew O'Bryan was watching his every move in his mirror, getting the same updates from his spotter and team on Dean's driving as he was getting on O'Bryan's. But he had twenty-plus years more experience than the younger man, twenty-plus seasons of tricks up his sleeve. Almost five hundred more races under his belt.

He was nearly twice O'Bryan's age, as Patsy kept pointing out. Twice as old, maybe, but more than twice as experienced, too.

Lapped traffic moved out of their way as they rocketed past at 160 miles an hour. Heading in to the far turn Dean made a move to the low side of the track but O'Bryan anticipated it and dropped down almost to the apron.

Two more laps ticked away with two more failed attempts to pass the race leader. Dean considered the option of trying to take him on the high side and discarded it. Time was too short, only four laps to go now. Behind him Shakey Paulson had dropped back to fifth and Kent and Justin Murphy were battling it out for third and fourth place.

Too far behind him to be of any drafting help. Once more they headed into the far turns, and then he saw his opening. O'Bryan was running a little higher in the groove this time giving him just enough of an opening. Dean feigned a run at O'Bryan's right rear bumper. Anticipating just that move, the younger driver veered slightly higher on the track and Dean, at last seeing the opening he needed, slammed his foot down on the accelerator and shot past on the inside.

He was in the lead. He was going to win the race.

But not the championship.

It had all come down to this. He would have another NASCAR win under his belt. But he would not win the title. He'd end up second or third in the points. Lose the championship—and his wife.

Because he was not going to call it a career unless he went out a champion.

AHEAD OF HIM Justin saw Dean Grosso and Rafael O'Bryan fighting it out for the lead, saw them seesaw, through the turns as they jockeyed for position, watched as the older man laid back on the straightaways letting O'Bryan cut the heavy air ahead of him before making his next run. They were down to three laps to go, the field strung out behind them. Shakey had dropped back to fifth place with a bad engine vibration but looked like he'd be able to finish the race. Hart Hampton had given up trying to hold his damaged race car together and headed for the garage. The remainder of the field was bunched up behind them.

He was racing Kent Grosso flat out and had been for the last eight laps. Justin wasn't certain where the hell Grosso had come from. Last he'd checked he'd been a lap down. Rafael O'Bryan must have let Sophia's brother back on the lead lap a while back. Grosso was well liked. Any number of drivers would give him a break, especially when none of them was racing for the NASCAR Sprint Cup Series championship themselves.

Then he saw it. O'Bryan drifting just a few feet farther on the high side than he had on the laps before. Dean Grosso moved as if he meant to bump O'Bryan's car up the track, but O'Bryan swerved to counter an attack that never came as the wily veteran slid past him on the inside and accelerated into the straightaway.

O'Bryan got a little loose as the disruption of Dean's car rocketing past disturbed the airflow around his car. His back end swerved as his tires lost their grip on the race track. The nose of the car headed for the wall. Justin shot a look out through the netting at Kent Grosso's cockpit as he braced himself for a possible collision with the other car. Kent was up on the wheel, staying low in the groove waiting for just that moment. As Justin watched, Sophia's brother slid by O'Bryan as he fought to right his car. The younger Grosso managed it just as they entered the far Turn Two abreast, Justin ran up close to O'Bryan's rear bumper again and waited for his chance.

He knew the numbers, knew that if O'Bryan finished the race where he was running now he'd still win, beating Dean Grosso out of the championship by a handful of points. But if Justin could pull off the same move Sophia's father had, he could put O'Bryan out of the running, and move himself into the top five in the points standings.

But could he do it before they ran out of race? There were only two laps left and O'Bryan wasn't going to be as easy to fool the second time. Justin tucked himself in behind his season-long rival and waited for just the right moment, letting O'Bryan cut the air ahead of him, drafting in his wake. Twice he feinted to the low side but O'Bryan held to his line and didn't take the bait.

But Justin wasn't out of tactics yet. He'd been watching the best of the best, the Grossos, father and son, and he'd picked up a trick or two of his own. That's why, when O'Bryan came up on the track to pass a lapped car staying on the low side, Justin stood on the gas and surged past him, his right side just inches from the wall. He pulled even with the former champion on the straightaway just in time to see Dean Grosso take the checkered flag. Two wide they rounded the final turn, O'Bryan clinging to the low groove but he was running flat out and Justin just kept coming. He had the engine. He had the car. He slammed the accelerator to the firewall.

They screamed down the front stretch and across the finish line nose-to-nose, but Justin knew it had been enough. Knew the sensors embedded in the track and the cars, the cameras stationed at the start-finish line, would tell the tale. He had beaten O'Bryan by the width of an eyelash.

A fraction of a second but it was enough. He would finish the points race in fifth place.

And Dean Grosso would win the NASCAR Sprint Cup Series championship.

Maybe now they would accept him into the dynasty, the family.

Sophia's family.

The one power on earth that could still keep them apart.

DEAN'S WORLD CHANGED in the space of a dozen heartbeats. He saw Kent come barreling across the finish line ahead of Rafael O'Bryan in his mirror. He was proud of his son coming from a lap down with less than fifty miles to go to finish second. He knew that Kent had made that final pass of O'Bryan to give him his best chance at the championship, but it wasn't enough. If O'Bryan finished third he'd still be the points winner. No one else had a chance to pass him but Justin Murphy, and Dean wasn't sure the younger driver had a car up to the challenge.

As he took his bittersweet victory lap other cars were passing him, giving him thumbs-up signs, shaking their fists. The buzz of voices in his earphones had risen to a level just below a scream. He couldn't understand a word anyone said. He crossed the start-finish line and spun his car in circles in the winner's traditional burnout. White smoke filled the air, some of it drifting into the cockpit partially obscuring his vision as he righted the car and headed toward Victory Lane.

He expected to see Rafael O'Bryan executing the same maneuver as he headed for the second winner's circle, the stage that had been set up especially for the awarding of the NASCAR Sprint Cup Series championship. But he was alone on the track.

His radio crackled to life. Roy-Bob was screaming from atop the grandstand. His crew chief was laughing in his ear, talking over his excited spotter. Someone ran out on to the track carrying a huge flag—the championship flag—heading straight for him.

He glanced at the leader board and saw the finish numbers. The No. 448 car stood in third position. Justin Murphy had somehow overtaken O'Bryan in the last few hundred feet of the race, in the last second of racing—and given the championship to Dean.

He stared up at the scoring pylon. Murphy had done it, passed O'Bryan in a slingshot move at the last possible instant. He wondered for a moment if he was hallucinating, but the whoops and hollers of celebration coming through his earphones told him what he saw had actually happened.

He was the NASCAR Sprint Cup Series champion.

And he owed it in part to the son of the man whose ghost had haunted his family for almost thirty years. That was a hell of a kick in the pants, but at the moment he didn't care. He dropped the safety net on the driver's side window and accepted the championship flag from the grinning official and set out on his second victory lap.

Twenty-five years he'd waited for this day. Seven hundred races, hundreds of thousands of miles strapped into the molded seat, enduring the stink and heat of a steel cage, sitting behind an engine so powerful only forces beyond his knowledge kept it from blowing itself to pieces every time he stepped on the gas. But none of that mattered now. Thousands of screaming fans were on their feet, waving, hats flying in the air.

He circled the track again, grinning like a fool, the wind tugging at the flag in his hand, longing for a deep cold drink of water, dead tired in every bone but still wired with adrenaline. He wouldn't sleep tonight, not for a long, long time. There were ceremonies and the hat dance and interviews that would last hours, a late-night flight home before he made it to his bed.

But would he be alone when he finally got there?

He had never envisioned this day without Patsy at his side. Would she be there for him tonight? She had walked him to his car as she had for a quarter of a century. She had stood beside him while they shared a moment of silent prayer. But, except for the kiss on the cheek at the press conference, she hadn't touched him. Hadn't kissed him. She had only laid her hand on his arm, wished him luck and disappeared back behind the pit wall not to be seen again.

His radio crackled to life in his ear once more. "Head on in to Victory Lane," his crew chief ordered. "They're going to combine the ceremonies."

Roy-Bob's laughter overrode Perry's instructions. "You screwed up the game plan, boy. O'Bryan was supposed to win the big one, get the giant cardboard check and the fireworks. But age and guile trumped his ace. They've got a stage set up on a flatbed down the way. It looks like a mob scene over there. Camera crews trampling each other to get back to Victory Lane. What a sight, buddy. You're missin' all the fun. Git your scrawny butt on down there. I've been waitin' a long time for this day."

So had he. But he had never expected to be celebrating it alone.

THEY WANTED Patsy on the podium with him. Wanted her to stand by Dean as he was presented with the huge cardboard check. They wanted to know how she felt to be both the wife and mother of a NASCAR Sprint Cup Series champion. Wanted to know how they all planned to celebrate now the season was over. *What was she supposed to say to that one? We're not going to Disney World? We're going to go home and file for divorce?* Her cheeks ached from smiling. Her head ached from all the noise and the tension. Her heart ached from being so close to Dean and yet feeling as if they resided in different universes.

"Kent, get your mother back to the motor home. This place isn't going to settle down for another hour at least," Dean said, breaking her muddled thoughts, pulling her back into the pandemonium that still reigned in Victory Lane. He leaned close to both of them so that they could hear each other, but not be overheard by the circling media.

"I'm fine," she said stubbornly. But she wasn't. She wanted desperately to be somewhere quiet and private. She couldn't keep up the happy facade a moment longer or she would begin to cry.

"You're going," Dean said in that maddeningly final way of his. She stiffened her spine, ready to argue as she seemed prone to do so often these days, but he disarmed her with his next words. "Wait for me at the motor home, Patsy, please," he said laying his hand on her arm. "Don't run away."

"Dean—" Lord, how was it possible to conduct your private life with so many people around, so many reporters alert and hungry for any tidbit of private happiness or strife.

"The plane leaves in an hour. Come home with me." She saw the emotion in his dark eyes, the knowledge that this time, this moment, was what they'd worked for and strived for all their lives together. He didn't want to spend it alone. She didn't want him to be alone. *She didn't want to be alone.*

"What about your grandparents. I'd planned to see they were all packed up before I leave."

"I'll take care of them," Kent said, urging her away. "Here comes the guy from the Sports Racing Network. Let's go."

Kent jumped down off the lower level of the podium and turned around, arms raised to catch her.

"I'll be there as soon as I can get away," Dean promised just as the huge trophy was thrust into his hands once more for another round of photographs, this time with Alan Cargill and his son, who had flown in for the race that morning.

They'd almost made their way to the gate leading back to the garages when a slightly plump young woman with a microphone moved directly into their path.

"Please, Mrs. Grosso. I'm with the South Florida Community College radio station. Would you please give me an interview. Just a short one."

Kent squeezed her arm and she knew he was prepared to deflect the girl's attention, but Patsy didn't have the heart to deny her, although her head ached and her stomach was tied in so many knots the flock of butterflies that usually took up residence there during a race couldn't get airborne. "What would you like to know?"

"How do you all intend to celebrate Dean's championship? I mean he's been trying to win for a long, long time." Since before recorded history, her tone implied. Patsy grinned; she couldn't help it. So young. So starry-eyed. So much to learn. "That one's easy. We'll all sit down together and share one of my husband's grandmother's fabulous Italian meals. We'll probably watch a tape of the race and my son and my husband and his grandfather will dissect every lap. Just as we did last year when Kent won the championship."

But would they really celebrate that way? She

doubted it. Things were very different this year than they had been just twelve short months ago.

"That sounds wonderful. How about you, Kent? What's next for you."

"We're going to celebrate just like my mom said. And then we're going to celebrate again for Thanksgiving and then we're off to New York for Champions Week and somewhere in there my fiancée and I are going to plan our wedding. Now if you'll excuse us, my mom and I want to get back to my great-grandparents and have some quiet time together."

"Sure. Sure. Thanks." The young reporter turned to her companion and threw her arms around her. "I'm going to ace this class! I got an interview with Patsy Grosso and an exclusive from Kent Grosso on his upcoming marriage!"

Kent rolled his eyes and began moving them toward the gate once more. "I'd better get together with Tanya and come up with a firm date. I don't doubt that whole interview will show up on the Internet before we're wheels up and out of here."

"You're probably right."

"Mom! Kent!" Sophia came dancing up to them. "Have I got any chance of getting to Dad?" she asked, grasping Patsy by the hands.

Patsy laughed and shook her head. "I doubt it. He's surrounded and right in the middle of the hat dance."

Sophia's bright smile dimmed a little. "Rats."

"We're just heading back to the motor homes to celebrate a little with Nana and Milo."

"I'll come, too," Sophia said, falling into step beside them as they headed toward the Cargill hauler where the sounds of celebrating were slightly more muted than they were in Victory Lane. "Justin's giving interviews. He moved up more places in the points standing than any of the other drivers," she said proudly. "Next year he'll win the championship."

"A year's a long way off," Kent said jokingly as they found their golf cart near the hauler, which was already being readied for the trip back to North Carolina.

"You'll see," Sophia said as they piled in Patsy's cart and headed back to the motor homes. "Justin will be a NASCAR champion, too, just like you and Dad."

"Dad might have something to say about that if he decides to defend—" Kent said and then abruptly stopped talking. "Sorry, Mom," he said. "I wasn't thinking—"

"It's all right, Kent. Your father and I have more issues than his staying on the circuit." That was true, but none of the other things that bothered her seemed as insurmountable as that one issue.

They were quiet until they reached Milo and Juliana's place. Once inside Patsy worked hard to appear in good spirits. Juliana took a tray of simple vegetable and cheese appetizers from the refrigerator and stirred up a pitcher of champagne punch. Kent and Milo watched the closed-circuit feed of the rest of the hat dance and a few more interviews with Dean and his crew chief and Alan Cargill while the sounds of departing motor homes rumbling past reminded them all that they would be leaving soon, too, another season behind them.

"We're not flying out with you," Juliana announced, popping a wedge of red bell pepper topped with a dollop of smoky-flavored cheese into her mouth. "We're going to ride back with Jesse in Kent's motor home. I have a huge amount of cooking to do for Thanksgiving and I'm going to have him stop in at a couple of specialty markets in Georgia and South Carolina on the way back."

"I wish I could join you, Nana," Sophia said longingly. "But I'm tapped out on days off. I don't want to miss any of the stuff going on in New York. I have to hitch a ride on the first plane going."

"We're leaving in an hour," Kent informed her. "Tanya's at the motor home now packing a few things she doesn't want to be without. Can you be ready to go that soon?"

"Sure can. Is there room for Justin?" she asked.

Kent glanced in Milo's direction, but the old man was absorbed, or pretended to be, watching Dean raise the elaborate championship trophy over his head once more as he exited Victory Lane. "Tell him to meet us at the helipad."

"Thanks, Kent."

"Hey, what's a big brother for?"

"To treat his sister like a princess."

"I've been doing that for twenty-eight years," he said with a bow that should have looked ridiculous but didn't. Patsy smiled, enjoying the banter between her children, wondering as always with a tiny part of her heart what it would be like to have two beautiful daughters standing side by side teasing their handsome brother.

"And you've almost got it right." She laughed. "I'm going to give Justin a call." Sophia slid a look sideways at Milo. "On second thought I'll run over to his trailer and give him the word in person. I'll be back in five minutes, so I don't miss Dad's entrance with the trophy. Got your camera, Nana?"

"Ready," she called out, busy refilling the appetizer tray. "I wonder if he'll bring anyone with him? Alan, of course. Any of the others?"

"Probably not, Nana," Kent said, helping himself to the replenished tray. "Larry and Crystal have already left. Steve and Heidi are leaving in a few minutes. Everyone's scrambling to get on the planes and get back home."

"I imagine you're right, although I talked to a couple of people who are planning to stay down here over Thanksgiving." Juliana sounded as though she couldn't imagine such a thing as not wanting to spend Thanksgiving in your own home, in your own kitchen, cooking from morning to night for two days straight.

The door opened and Dean entered carrying the NASCAR Sprint Cup Series championship trophy, silver folds resembling checkered flags designed by Tiffany and weighing as much as a year-old child. *His heart's desire. His to keep forever.* He was still wearing his uniform, damp in spots from the champagne sprayed all around Victory Lane, grinning from ear to ear. He lifted the trophy slightly above his head, then walked directly to where his grandfather was sitting.

"I did it, Milo," he said and Patsy's heart contracted at the emotion in his voice. "I finally did it."

Milo unfolded himself slowly from his chair, straightened to his full height, held out his hand to touch the symbol of stock car racing's pinnacle, a milestone he'd never reached in his driving career. "Congratulations, son," he said, tears of pride filling his faded brown eyes as he placed his hand on Dean's arm. "I knew you'd bring it home someday. I've always had faith in you."

"Thanks." Dean handed the gleaming trophy to Kent and swept Juliana into a hug. "What will we do with the thing, Nana?" he asked her as she tearfully hugged him back."

"I have no idea," she said. "Could we use it for a punch bowl?"

"That's a possibility. Maybe over the holidays."

"There's a case at the garage ready and waiting for it," Patsy reminded him as Sophia, who had returned just moments before Dean's arrival, reached out to run her hand along the edge of the shining metal.

"That case's been empty way too long, Patsy-girl," he said, grinning wickedly, locking his gaze to hers.

"Way too long," she agreed, her breath quickening as it had for over thirty years when he smiled at her that way.

"Thank goodness it's going to the garage. I certainly don't want to have to think about keeping it polished," Juliana said, picking up her camera, wiping tears from her eyes. "Come. Everyone. Gather 'round," she commanded. "I want to get a family picture before you scatter to the four winds."

Patsy felt a little shiver of foreboding run across her skin. A family picture. An ordinary enough way to celebrate a momentous occasion. Except if she stayed on the course she'd set for herself, if Dean didn't agree to retire now that he'd completed his quest for the NASCAR Sprint Cup Series championship, it would most likely be their last.

CHAPTER THIRTEEN

DEAN HANDED PATSY A glass of champagne. He'd never really liked sparkling wine, especially after so many years of having it sprayed in his eyes. The damned stuffed burned like fire. He was a shot-and-beer kind of guy himself, but he'd learned to drink the fancy stuff, and even appreciate it. Just like he'd learned to give interviews with quotable sound bites, learned to shake hands for hours on end with flashbulbs going off in his face, learned to make small talk with fans that didn't encourage lingering but conveyed the fact that he appreciated their support and cared about what they thought of him. And he'd learned to take care of his sponsors. Above all else the sponsor came first.

But not tonight. Tonight he was on a mission to win back the woman he loved. "Fly home with me," he said as she reached for the flute of sparkling wine. "Please."

Her hand trembled but her words were firm and clear. "I'm thinking of flying back with Kent."

He reached out and curled his hand around her wrist, oblivious to the voices of the others swirling around them as they posed for snapshots with the NASCAR Sprint Cup Series championship trophy and each other. "Not tonight, Patsy. Stay with me. This is what we worked toward all these years. Can't we put aside our differences for a little while to enjoy it?"

She looked down at his hand on hers, looked up into his eyes. "I don't think it's a good idea," she said but her tone wasn't as convincing as before.

"Patsy, please. I'm not asking to move back into the house." He took a breath, swallowed his pride. "I don't want to be alone. Not tonight."

She was quiet a moment, considering. He braced himself for her refusal but instead she said, "I'll fly back with you." Her eyes were dark with uncertainty and he knew she hadn't changed her mind about the divorce but now he had hope. Kent's cell phone beeped. Patsy broke eye contact and slid her hand from his light grasp. "But that's all I'm promising, do you understand?"

"Yes," he said, the spark of hope her agreement had ignited threatening to die away. "I understand."

"That was Tanya," Kent announced. "The helicopter radioed that they're about ten minutes out. We need to get a move on." He held out his hand to Dean. "Congratulations again, Dad. You finally got what you deserved from this business."

Dean grasped his son's hand and then pulled him into a bear hug. "Couldn't let you outdo me, son. Had to keep the cup in the family."

"And out of the hands of those good-for-nothing Murphys," Milo muttered.

Silence stretched out for a couple of beats after the old man's utterance. Dean saw a look of strain cross Juliana's face and was shocked for a moment at how old the unguarded expression made her look. She wasn't a young woman anymore, he realized suddenly. She was always so vibrant and energetic it was hard to remember sometimes she was well into her seventies.

"Justin Murphy did me a big favor tonight when he passed O'Bryan and Rafael finished out of the money. If he hadn't made that last move, O'Bryan would be trying to figure out a place to display this baby alongside his other one." Dean gave the trophy a tap with the end of his finger. He saw the look of gratitude on Sophia's face from the corner of his eye, but it was the sadness, the resignation in her blue eyes, so like Patsy's, that twisted his heart and made him suddenly impatient with his grandfather's intransigence.

His daughter was in love with Justin Murphy and the family's, especially Milo's, continued animosity toward the boy was causing her great heartache. That was unacceptable. He had his own axe to grind with the Murphys, old scores still to be settled, but he could put his anger aside for Sophia's sake, he'd known that all along. He could live with a black mark against his character in regards to Troy Murphy's mysterious death, but not his baby's sadness.

But how in hell were they going to bring the old man around? As long as the deaths of Troy and Connor Murphy went unsolved there would be no chance of burying the past for the sake of the next generation's future.

He looked past Sophia to her mother, saw his thoughts mirrored in her eyes. Maybe ensuring their daughter's happiness would be a bridge he could build to cross the divide that separated them. It was sure as hell worth a try.

"Sophia. We need to leave now," Kent urged his sister.

"I'm ready," she said. "Nana. Grandpa, see you back home," she said giving them both a quick hug and kiss on the cheek. "Mom, you and Dad fly safe." She repeated the embraces, and hurried out the door Kent was holding open for her.

Patsy and Juliana followed them outside. Dean waited for Milo to negotiate the steep steps then joined them in the cool evening air. All around them motor homes were being buttoned up and moved out of the lot. The smell of diesel fuel hung heavily in the air. The race was long over now, the traffic cleared away so that the big units could head out onto the highway and points north and west without too much difficulty or delay.

Figures moved around in the shadows as storage compartments were opened and closed, golf carts and "toads," cars that would be hauled behind the big units, were being guided onto their tow bars. Now and then one of the motor home drivers called out a greeting, offered Dean congratulations. He waved and nodded and thanked them all.

A man wearing faded jeans and a leather jacket detached himself from the darker shadows and walked toward them, a small duffle slung over one shoulder. It was Justin Murphy. When she caught sight of him Sophia cast a quick glance in her great-grandparents' direction before moving forward to meet him. She took his hand but didn't give him one of her exuberant hugs or even a kiss on the cheek. Once more Dean felt an overwhelming urge to protect his daughter from hurt, mixed with equal parts shame that his own hard feelings had blinded him to the real depth of Sophia's pain.

Well, there was no time like the present to make things right.

He stepped forward with his hand outstretched. "I want to thank you for what you did today. I wouldn't have won this if you hadn't got past O'Bryan on the last lap." He indicated the gleaming silver trophy sitting on the seat of the golf cart where he'd just finished placing it.

Justin hesitated for a moment, glancing first at Sophia and then quickly at Milo and Juliana, who were standing on Dean's left side. One or two more ticks of the clock passed in silence and then Justin reached out and pumped Dean's hand. "I mostly did it for myself," he said with a grin. "But I have to admit I hoped it might smooth over a few of the rough edges between us if I pulled it off."

"I think you accomplished both your goals," Dean said, trying not to wince at the unexpected strength of Justin's handshake. "Welcome to the family, son."

"Dean?" Patsy's tone was doubtful. "Are you sure—"

Dean grinned and pumped Justin's hand harder. "I'm sure. If my Sophia wants to marry into another racing family then I'm not going to stand in her way."

"Thank you, sir." This time Dean winced when Justin gripped his hand. He couldn't help it.

"Dad!" Sophia launched herself into his arms so forcefully he had to take a step back to keep his balance. "Thank you. Thank you." She was crying, just as she always did when she was happy or deeply touched. Kent slapped Justin on the back and took his turn shaking hands.

Patsy reached up on tiptoe and gave Justin a kiss. "Welcome to the family, Justin."

"Not so fast," Milo wheezed, moving into the circle, leaning heavily on his cane. Sophia and Juliana broke off the laughing hug they'd been sharing and turned to stare at the old man they both loved. "I can't stop my great-granddaughter from marrying you, Murphy, more's the pity, but don't ever think I'll welcome you into the family." He shook the cane in Justin's direction.

"Grandpa." Sophia's expression changed from joy to sadness. Her eyes were two huge wells of tears. "Please. Don't say such things."

"I mean it, Sophia. And he's not welcome in my home."

Her eyes narrowed and she lifted her chin, looking so much like her mother that Dean's throat clogged with emotion. "If Justin's not welcome at the farm then I won't be coming there, either."

"I didn't mean for you to stay away, Sophia," the old man said with a little less certainty.

"If the man I'm going to marry isn't welcome then neither am I."

"Milo." Juliana looked stricken. "Think of what you're saying."

"I know what I'm saying," the old man declared, hardening again. "I may be old but I still have my pride. He's a Murphy. They lie. They cheat. They steal. They ruin lives." His voice broke. "As long as I have breath in my body I won't change my mind." He turned and limped into the motor home, never looking back.

"Nana," Sophia whispered, stricken. "What have I done? What can I do?"

Juliana didn't answer for a moment, staring after her husband as he slammed the door and sealed himself inside, alone with his bitterness. When she turned back to them her expression was closed. "You haven't done anything but fall in love with a fine young man. Pay my husband no heed, Justin. He will change his mind. Sooner, rather than later. I promise you that." She walked over to where Justin stood with Sophia in his arms. She reached up on tiptoe and gave him a kiss on the cheek. "Go, take Sophia home."

"But Nana, Grandpa never goes back on his word," Sophia whispered. She shot Dean a beseeching look but at the moment there was nothing he could do to help her.

"He's upset," Juliana said, sounding exhausted all of a sudden.

"We'll settle this when we're all back home. Everyone's too tired and stressed out right now." Patsy reached out and touched Sophia's cheek, wiping away a tear just as she had done when Sophia was little and had scraped her knee or fallen off her bike. "Nana's right. We all need to cool off. It's been one hell of a day. We'll figure out some way to get Milo to see reason. It's the not knowing that's so hard on him." She flashed Justin an apologetic look. "If we only knew the real story behind the two of your kins' deaths we could put it all in the past where it belongs."

Justin's face was as hard as Milo's had been but his voice was resigned when he spoke. "I'm not sure of that, ma'am. I'm not sure of that at all."

THE FLIGHT BACK to Concord had been noisy and happy, a continuation of the day's celebrations. Alan and his son Nathan, Roy-Bob, Dean's Motor Media rep and a few close friends made the trip on Alan's corporate plane, the NASCAR Sprint Cup Series championship trophy belted into a seat of its own, the guest of honor.

Patsy had done her best to join in the merrymaking, the toasts to Dean, to his team, to Alan, even for her, but her heart wasn't in it. The scene outside the motor home continued to haunt her thoughts. What if Sophia meant what she said, that she and Justin wouldn't return to the farm until Milo recognized Justin as a member of the family? As stubborn as Milo was it could mean their estrangement for the rest of his life. Recognizing that possibility, she feared Sophia might break off her engagement to the man Patsy was certain her daughter loved with all her heart

Which of her daughter's choices would be the most painful, the hardest for her mother's heart to bear? She didn't know. Couldn't bear to contemplate either outcome. By the time the plane touched down at the airport just a few miles from the speedway that all three of the men in her life considered their home track, she was exhausted. All she wanted was to go home, shower and crawl into her bed. She said her goodbyes to Alan and his son, to the others on the plane. No one lingered. They scattered into the darkness looking for cars and trucks and vans to take them home to a well-deserved rest. The plane taxied into the night and almost for the first time in eighteen hours silence reigned all around her.

She started for her car but before she'd gone three

feet Dean appeared at her side and fell into step with her. "It's too late for you to be walking alone," he said when she made a sound of protest.

"I know," she agreed. "But I'm prepared. Sophia was insistent I have my pepper spray and my mini-air-horn key ring," she said, jingling the heavy key ring her daughter had given her shortly after Dean moved out in front of his face. "I'm not an easy target, mister. Any mugger that comes near me will wish he hadn't."

Dean laughed. "Looks formidable all right."

"It is. Want a demonstration of the horn?" she asked, giving him a sliding glance from the corner of her eye.

"No thanks. I'll take your word for it." He had deposited the trophy with Alan and his son for safe keeping and all he was carrying was a small duffel. He'd left everything else behind in the motor home, as she had, to be driven back from Miami.

They reached her car. She stopped for a moment before inserting the key in the lock. He was standing beside her, so close, closer than he'd been in weeks. He'd showered and shaved before they left the drivers' and owners' lot and she couldn't stop herself from breathing in his familiar scent, soap, and the spicy pine aftershave she'd given him on his birthday the year before…and warm, clean skin.

Her breathing quickened and she felt a little weak in the knees. It had been so long since they'd made love. She missed it. She missed him. But she would miss him far more if fate took him from her. She hardened her resolve but found it melting away even more quickly than she'd summoned it when his hand closed over hers and he took her keys away. "I'll drive you home, Patsy," he said. "Just like I used to all those years ago."

She didn't play coy or pretend she didn't understand the ramifications of getting into the car with him. "Oh, Dean, I don't think—"

He leaned down and kissed her, softly but thoroughly. "Shh," he said against her lips. "You think too much. C'mon, I've got a better idea. The truck's right over here. We'll take that instead. I'll just drive you out along the lake and we'll lie in the back and look up at the stars."

She laughed. She couldn't help herself. "Oh, no, you don't. In the first place it's November and it's cold. And in the second place every other time you tried that line on me we ended up doing all kinds of things but watch the stars."

"I know," he said in that low, sexy growl he reserved only for their lovemaking. "I remember each and every time, too." He plucked the keys from her nerveless fingers and pulled her into his arms, leaning back against her car. "Do you want me to describe them to you? The first time? The time the sheriff's car almost caught us in the act." His voice deepened, darkened. "Or the time we made Sophia. I'll never forget that night." He was nuzzling her neck, molding her to him and it felt so good. So very good.

Oh, God, she would never forget those magical nights, either. Never. But they were long in the past. They were older now. Life wasn't all in front of them, a wonderful challenge. She was afraid now to look too far into the future. "I don't think that's a very good idea," she managed to say in what she hoped wasn't too breathless a tone.

He frowned a moment, then set her away from him, took her hand and started walking through the nearly empty parking area beside the Cargill hanger toward his truck. "Okay. We won't talk about memories of what we did years ago. We'll go to the farm and we'll make some new ones tonight."

She tried to muster her resolve to tell him no, but she couldn't. She seemed momentarily to have lost the hurt and the fear that had driven her these past few months. His hand was warm and strong in hers. It felt right to have him walking beside her, the other half of her she'd missed so badly. Didn't what they had shared together for so long deserve another chance?

He found his pickup, opened the passenger door and lifted her up onto the seat as though she was still the willowy sixteen-year-old she'd once been. She laid her head against the backrest of the passenger seat and closed her eyes. What was she doing, she asked herself, making one more attempt to deal logically with a purely emotional situation? How had she let herself be manipulated this way? The answer was simple and came readily to mind. *Because she still loved him.* Her heart raced in her chest. Heaven help her, she was still so very much in love with him.

Dean started the big truck and put it into gear. He was so close, the heat from his thigh brushing against hers as he turned a corner burned through her clothing. With one hand on the wheel, his arm draped across the back of the seat, he moved them out into the sparse, late-night traffic and turned, heading toward Concord.

They were on their way to the farm. They were on their way home.

A wave of exhaustion washed over her. She fought the sleepiness for a moment then decided to give in to it, but not before she'd made her position plain to the man beside her. "Just because I'm letting you come home with me doesn't mean things are settled between us. It's just that tonight's a very important night for you."

"For us," he said, still in that private sexy growl. A shiver ran over her skin and she rubbed her hand up her arm to ease the prickling before it could move deeper into her body, turn into desire and take away her resolve.

"For us," she agreed, looking straight ahead. "I've missed you. I've missed making love to you. But I haven't changed my mind about anything. If you aren't going to retire from racing, then in the morning you'll have to leave. I may not be strong enough to get out of this truck and walk away from you right now but I will be tomorrow."

CHAPTER FOURTEEN

THE BEDSIDE CLOCK indicated it was morning but the sun had not yet risen and dawn was still just a faint lightening in the eastern sky beyond their bedroom window. Patsy lay awake in the darkness, listening to Dean's gentle snoring, luxuriating in the feel of him snuggled close against her, the weight of his arm strong and comforting across her stomach.

She turned a little so that she could look at his face. She didn't need daylight to make out the familiar planes and angles, the lines at the corners of his eyes etched there from years of sun and wind and speed; the scar at the corner of his left eyebrow that he'd gotten while trimming the big magnolia tree in the front yard when a branch had snapped unexpectedly and almost knocked him off the ladder. Temptation overtook her and she reached out to trace the small crescent shape with the tip of her finger. He had other scars, some from racing accidents, but she didn't search those out. She didn't want to think about racing, not right now. Not this moment.

They had made love passionately, hungrily, but wordlessly. It was as if their coming together was as fragile as the truce they'd called for this one night.

Losing herself to further temptation, she ran her hand over the dark hair on his chest. It was soft and springy, sprinkled with more gray than the dark brown hair on his head. Their lovemaking hadn't solved the problems between them but maybe it had given them the chance to discuss them once more? They had been through so much together over the years. The good. The bad. The almost unendurable when their baby was stolen and lost to them forever. But they had always worked through those problems and come out stronger on the other side.

Could they do it one more time?

His hand came up, covered hers. He had gone from sound asleep to fully awake in an instant. She had always marveled at his ability to do that. She hated waking up. Even when the children had been babies and some small part of her was always on alert, she had found it hard to shake off the lethargy of sleep in so short a space of time.

"Good morning," he said, giving her a kiss.

"Good morning," she whispered back.

"Ready for breakfast?" he asked. He was relaxed now. The focused intensity of a professional driver, the tension and excitement that had seethed below the surface yesterday after he had won the race and the NASCAR Sprint Cup Series championship, had drained away with their lovemaking. Now he looked totally satisfied and well rested.

She was well rested and very satisfied herself, too, she thought. "Mmm, in another hour or two," she said. They had made love with an abandon they hadn't experienced in years. She felt whole and complete again. She felt like a woman not burdened with a lot of adjectives to describe her: a woman of a certain age, a mother of grown children, someone fast approaching her fiftieth birthday. Simply a woman who was loved by a caring man, no longer so afraid of what tomorrow might bring, she was willing to spend the rest of her life only half alive to be spared any more pain.

"You can go back to sleep in a few minutes. First I want to make love to you again."

"I have to go into the garage," she said. It wasn't much of an excuse and she knew it. "Just because you won the Cup doesn't mean I don't have work to do."

"I like the kind of work you're doing now," he said, bending his head to nuzzle her ear. "I think you should take it up full-time."

She laughed a little, but it had a breathless quality to it. "I might get used to it," she said, kissing the edge of his mouth, the line of his jaw. "If it pays well enough."

He gathered her into his arms, his voice rough with urgency and need. "Anything you want. Anything at all."

She wanted him with her every hour of every day for the rest of their lives. She wanted to say those words aloud, make him give her his unbreakable pledge he would abide by the bargain, but before she could voice her wishes his mouth came down on hers once more. Patsy forgot all the ultimatums she had made over the past few months. Forgot the hurt and the anxiety and the dread that had haunted her day and night. All she wanted now was what they were sharing once more after so long a time alone.

She wanted Dean. And she had him. And all was right with the world.

THE ALARM WENT OFF at seven, just as it always did. He woke to find himself in his own bed with Patsy curled up beside him.

It wasn't a dream. He hadn't died and gone to heaven. He was home and he had made love to his wife, again and again, just as they had when they were so much younger than they were today.

He had her back.

And he had the NASCAR Sprint Cup Series championship trophy.

He rolled over and put his hands behind his head, smiling at the still shadowed ceiling. He had it all. And he was damned well going to keep it this time. He wasn't deluded enough to believe that last night had solved everything that was wrong between them. He knew Patsy still harbored doubts and fears about his future in NASCAR. Could he give her what she wanted now that he had obtained the goal he'd set for himself so many years ago?

Could he retire, get out from behind the wheel and move exclusively into the corporate aspects of the sport he loved almost as much as he loved the woman beside him? It wouldn't be easy. He didn't kid himself that it would. It would take a hell of a lot of determination, but he could do it. The alternative wasn't to be considered. He wasn't going to spend the next thirty years of his life without the woman he loved. Not for a hundred NASCAR Sprint Cup Series championships.

The phone rang and he grabbed the receiver. "Dean. I've been trying to reach you. Your cell's not answering." It was his PR rep.

"Sorry, Jane," he said. "I guess I let the battery run down." He wondered how Jane had known to find him here? Then he figured probably everyone on the plane had seen they were headed for a reconciliation.

"I just wanted to remind you that you have those radio interviews to do for the early morning drive time. The first one's up in ten minutes."

"I'll do them from here," Dean said, swinging his legs over the side of the bed.

"I can work that for you. Just keep this line clear."

"Will do," he assured her. "Thanks for giving me the heads-up. I'll be ready."

"Just doing my job. Will you be at the farm for the rest of the day?" she asked after a little hesitation. "You're doing the late night talk show appearance tonight remember. I'll send a car to take you to the airport if you want."

He thought about it a moment, the temptation of a few hours here was a strong one but he decided against that plan. "No. I'll be at the garage. The car can pick me up there, the way we planned it last night."

"Got ya. I'll get off the line so you can get ready for the radio gigs."

He wasn't crazy about flying to New York to tape a segment of the popular late night talk show but there was no way he could beg off. It was part of his job. Part of being the NASCAR champ. But he wasn't about to face the suits in the Big Apple alone. "Jane, you're coming to New York with me, aren't you?"

"You bet ya. It's my job to make you look good, remember?" she said, laughing. "Congratulations again, Dean. It's been great working with you."

"We're not done yet," he reminded her with a grin. "Not by a long shot."

"Not done with what?" Patsy asked. Even before he caught sight of the slight frown she wore in her reflection in the mirror on the wall at the foot of their bed he heard it in her voice.

"With this Cup gig," he said, reaching for his jeans and pulling them on. "In fact it's just starting. I've got to hit the bathroom and get some clothes on. The drive-time radio interviews start in ten minutes. There's no way I'm talking to those guys in the altogether."

That tickled her. She started to laugh and the frown flitted away. She was sitting against the pillows, the sheet up to her chin to counteract the early morning chill and Dean wanted nothing more than to drop back down on the mattress beside her and take her in his arms.

She read his thoughts. "Go," she said, waving him away. "Get cleaned up and decent. I'll make us some coffee and bring it in to you."

"Will you come to New York with me?" he asked suddenly. He would only be in the city for a few hours. It was madness to ask her to make the long tiring trip without even the enticement of shopping or the theater.

She shook her head. "No. I have work to do, remember?" She glanced at the bedside clock. "And now it's half an hour later than it was the first time I said it."

She was frowning, just a little, a small furrow between her softly shaped eyebrows. He loved kissing her there, following the arch with his lips, with his fingertips. He sat down beside her.

"We need to talk, Patsy-girl," he said softly, aware as she was that the clock was ticking, that they had so little time together to say so very much. "About us. About what's coming up."

"I know," she said.

"We need to decide where we're going. What we want to do with the second half of our lives."

"But all the other things are peripheral to the most important one."

"I know," he said. "Will I retire or not?"

She nodded. It looked as if she were holding her breath as she waited for his answer.

"I love you more than anything in this world, Patsy-girl. I lost sight of that for a little while chasing down the championship this season. If you want me to stop driving. I'll do it."

She put her hands in front of her mouth for a moment, her eyes filling with tears. "Would you have said that if you hadn't won the championship last night?" she asked.

He gave her a rueful grin. "I like to think I would have. But it would take a hell of a lot more willpower to keep my word," he said. He had never lied to her before, and he wasn't going to start today.

"I wouldn't have believed you if you'd told me anything different." She threw her arms around his neck and rubbed her forehead against his. "Oh, Dean. I'm sorry I've been acting so foolishly. It's just that I think when Sophia found her courage to come and watch you and Kent and Justin race, I lost mine. I want to spend every day of the rest of my life with you," she said, her voice catching on the words.

"So do I, Patsy-girl. So do I." He bent his head and kissed her, holding her close.

She lifted her mouth from his and pushed him gently away. "The interviews. You've got five minutes left to get ready. We have the rest of our lives to talk."

"That we do, Patsy-girl."

SHE COULDN'T BELIEVE what was happening. Could it all be coming back together so easily? Could Dean really walk away from what he did best? What he had done for almost thirty years without looking back, without regret?

She found herself staring down at two empty mugs on a bamboo tray. What had she meant to do with them?

"Coffee, silly," she said aloud. "You were making coffee for your husband."

She was standing at the counter of their small kitchen situated directly above Juliana's much larger one, spooning coffee grounds into the basket of the coffeemaker, buttering toast, searching for the creamer while Dean gave radio interviews to half a dozen sports stations over the phone.

He had told her he would retire now that he had won the NASCAR Sprint Cup Series championship. They would go back to being a team. Husband and wife. Patsy and Dean. A couple. She wouldn't have to spend the rest of her life without him.

She kept smiling while she worked. Her hands

were shaking, she noticed, surprised. She felt as giddy as a bride. He would be with her from now on. He would be there to talk his grandfather into accepting Justin and Sophia's marriage. He would be with her to grumble about the expense and extravagance of their daughter's wedding. They could exercise their option to buy out Alan Cargill and take over Cargill Motors—Cargill-Grosso Racing—as they'd planned months before.

She felt a little weak in the knees. She hadn't realized how desperately she missed him until she had him back. They would go to sleep together and they would wake up together and she would never, ever have to watch him strap himself into the seat of a race car again.

She picked up the tray and carried it into their bedroom. Dean was sitting on the edge of the bed, barefoot, shirtless, yesterday's beard darkening his chin. He was talking to some radio personality or another.

She was only half paying attention to what Dean was saying. She'd folded a couple of bright yellow napkins in triangles, added some of Juliana's to-die-for peach jam in a little crystal dish, covered the toast and English muffins with another napkin and added an insulated carafe of coffee. Her stomach growled. Lovemaking always made her hungry. With any luck they could spend half the morning in bed.

"Buddy, I'll tell you straight up. I knew I could win the race. I intended to win the race. The team worked well together. My crew chief called a heck of a race. The Smoothtone Music people are the best sponsors a driver could have. But winning the Cup wasn't in my control. Thank the Lord everything lined up just right. I got some help when I needed it and came away with the championship. What more can I say?"

He looked over his shoulder, telephone pressed to his ear, and smiled at her as if they were alone in the universe. She smiled back, sat the tray down on the bedside table and started around the bed to sit beside him. And then in less time that it took to move that short distance everything changed again.

"Buddy, it's way too early for me to be thinking about next season," she heard Dean say, his voice a shade less jovial, a little strained. "I'm enjoying myself. I'm enjoying being an owner but I'm not done driving. Not just yet. I have a championship to defend, don't I?"

He wasn't looking at her, but straight ahead out the window that overlooked the pasture where Milo's horses grazed.

She couldn't believe what she was hearing. Couldn't believe he was telling the interviewer, a man she now recognized as a former driver—with an audience of close to a *million* listeners—that he was not retiring. That he intended to come back and defend his title.

He had lied to her.

He had no intention of keeping his promise to her.

Reality jolted through her. He had broken his promise to her, so now she would be forced to keep the one she had made—to divorce him.

"PATSY, FOR GOD'S sake what's the matter now?" It was half an hour later. Dean must have finished his interviews because he'd followed her downstairs to Juliana's unusually quiet and empty kitchen.

"What's the matter?" she asked, not turning away from the big sink where she was staring listlessly down at the drain. She didn't even have any dirty dishes to wash to keep her hands busy. She rested her palms on the cold surface of the apron-fronted sink and bowed her head. "You lied to me, that's what's the matter. Or don't you remember just an hour ago promising me that you were going to retire?"

"I did tell you that, yes," he said warily.

He hadn't taken the time to shower or shave. He'd pulled on his shirt but hadn't bothered to button it or to find his shoes. "Yet you told Buddy Trimble that you can't wait to come back next season."

"Yes, I did," he said, stalking toward her but stopping on the other side of Juliana's big work island, staying out of reach, out of her space.

"You told all the others the same thing."

He nodded. "I did," he said, his eyes narrowing. "Surely you know why?" he insisted.

She turned, holding her head high, keeping tight rein on her emotions. The effort made her voice sound strident and hard but she couldn't help that. It was hard enough just getting the words out without breaking into tears. "No. I don't know why," she said. "All I know is you lied to me."

He pounded his fist on the granite countertop, making her jump. "Good Lord, woman. Stop and think a moment."

Patsy stared at him, stunned. She seldom saw Dean lose his temper but he was angry now. Her own anger flared. What right had he to be mad at her? He was the one who had broken his solemn promise to her, a promise sealed with their lovemaking, not the other way around. "I have been thinking, Dean," she said, coming away from the sink to face him across the island. "I think I made a very big mistake last night letting you back into my bed—"

"Our bed," he growled, splaying both hands on the granite. "It's still our bed."

"Not anymore."

His eyes narrowed. "You're throwing me out?" he asked and she felt a little chill skitter across her nerve endings. He had never reacted this way before. He had never shown his own anger and pain so nakedly.

She nodded. "I never said you could stay," she reminded him.

He rounded the big island so quickly she had time to take only a single step backward before he reached out and took her by the arms. "Aren't you even going to ask me why I told Buddy and the others I was coming back to defend the Cup?" he asked.

"Because you want to race more than you want to be married to me," she said and hated the thread of self-pity she could hear in her words.

His eyes darkened, then emptied of anger and emotion. It was more frightening than any act of violence might have been because it signaled such finality. He dropped his hands from her arms and turned away. He shook his head. "Patsy, you're the smartest woman I know. Can't you see what I'm doing?"

"No" she said. "Tell me." She didn't even think he heard the pleading note in her voice.

He ran his hand through his hair, across his beard-roughened chin. "I can't just up and announce to the world I'm retiring without consulting Smoothtone Music. They've been my sponsors for twenty years. There are the endorsements. The other sponsors to consider. I can't quit driving without telling my team. Without talking to Alan. Patsy, we'll have everything we own tied up in Cargill-Grosso Racing if we go through with our deal to buy out Alan."

"I didn't—" Patsy felt her breath stop in her chest, constrict her throat and cut off any more words.

"A lot of people depend on us, Patsy. On me. We have to put a lot of thought into how we make the change." His eyes narrowed. "How I make the change from driver to owner." He threw up his hand, slapped it down on his thigh. "Hell, there was a time I wouldn't even have had to say all this aloud," he said, suddenly looking as exhausted as he had every right to be. "You would have read my mind. You would already have been two steps ahead of me. But we don't think like a team anymore. We don't work like a team anymore. I guess last night was just a kind last hurrah for us. Maybe you're right. Maybe it's best if we do go our separate ways."

CHAPTER FIFTEEN

"MEN ARE SUCH POOPS," Juliana said, upending her wineglass. "I should know. I've been married to one for forty-seven years."

"I agree," Patsy seconded. "They are put on this earth for no other purpose than to cause us grief and misery."

They were sitting around the little wrought-iron bistro table in Sophia's kitchen working on Juliana's Thanksgiving menu. It was a ritual they usually performed in the big kitchen at the farm. But not this year. Sophia still wouldn't step foot under Milo's roof without Justin and no amount of persuasion and, Patsy suspected, some gentle bullying on Juliana's part, had changed Milo's mind.

"Mom, Nana, I can't believe I'm hearing you right." Sophia glanced at her neighbor and best friend, Alicia Perez. Both of the younger women looked uncomfortable.

Uh-oh, Patsy thought. She doesn't want to hear her mother and great-grandmother talking about their problems with the men in their lives. It was time to change the subject, but after two glasses of wine Juliana was on a roll.

"I am fed up to my eyeteeth with their ultimatums and their crochets and most of all their bullheaded pride." Juliana, looking like a harvest goddess in layers of brown and orange and sparkling gold and copper jewelry, picked up one of the parmesan pesto sticks she was auditioning for her spectacular Thanksgiving antipasto plates, and bit down on it as though she were imagining doing something similar to her intractable husband's head.

"Nana." Sophia's eyes were big as saucers. Patsy motioned for Alicia to pour a touch more Chianti into her daughter's glass. All these female revelations were proving too much for Sophia. She needed to get a little drunk. Patsy shocked herself with the thought. When had she crossed the line from thinking of Sophia as her little girl to a woman who needed to get a little drunk? She wasn't sure when it had happened, sometime during this long, grueling season, but it had.

Alicia added a splash of wine to Sophia's glass. Juliana, held out her goblet, too. "Just a tad more, Alicia honey. I'm wound up tighter than a two-dollar watch and I'd rather have another glass of this nice wine than take a chill pill."

Sophia wasn't the only one who didn't want to know her loved ones were having trouble in their marriages. Patsy didn't like to hear that Juliana and Milo were at odds with one another. She downed the rest of her Chianti in one swallow and held out her glass for more. Shrugging, Alicia poured a few more ounces.

It was a week after the Homestead race, the Monday before Thanksgiving. Dean was meeting with his Smoothtone Music sponsors in Nashville and Patsy had no idea at all what he was telling them. Was he announcing his retirement or was he renegotiating a new contract with his long-time sponsor? She had no idea because they hadn't exchanged a single word in the past six days. She didn't even know if he planned to share Thanksgiving dinner with the family. He had walked out of the farm house one week ago and she hadn't seen or heard a word from him since.

Exactly what she had said she wanted him to do.

It was a sobering thought. Except she didn't need sobering up. She was already stone-cold sober and as miserable as she could be.

"I'm going to El Paso to spend Thanksgiving with my family," Alicia said, gamely attempting to steer the subject into safer waters. "My oldest sister and her husband just became grandparents. Twins," she said. "My nephew, Carlos, the babies' daddy, was my best friend growing up. He and his wife asked me to be godmother."

"How wonderful for you," Patsy said, genuinely pleased for Sophia's good friend. "What are the babies' names?" She liked thinking about being a grandmother. The prospect pleased her and now that both Kent and Sophia were in committed relationships she was more anxious than ever before to hold her grandchildren in her arms.

"Carmella Maria and Juan Carlos," Alicia said.

"Good strong names. "Juliana nodded approvingly. "I don't like all the foo-foo names people saddle babies with these days."

"I've always liked the name Gina," Sophia said a little dreamily as though her thoughts, too, might be centered on the grandbabies Patsy wished for. "Wasn't that my grandmother's name? Dad's mother. She was Gina, wasn't she?"

Patsy's hand tightened on the stem of her wineglass. She didn't dare glance at Dean's grandmother, didn't dare make eye contact with the older woman. They had not discussed Patsy's lost child in many years. It was a subject too painful for either of them to speak of dispassionately so they kept silent and mourned her in their hearts.

Juliana regained her composure first although Patsy saw her hand was trembling badly when she picked up a pencil to tick off another ingredient on her page-long shopping list. "Yes, it was. Such a pretty name, Angelina. She was a beautiful woman. Tall and slender, shining blond hair."

"I could use the tall and slender," Alicia said.

"And I wish I'd gotten some of the shining part of her blond hair," Sophia said, smiling at her friend. "My highlights are the work of my fantastic stylist. Maybe if Justin and I have a little girl someday we'll name her Gina. I think Dad would like that, don't you?"

"Yes," Patsy said, the thinly healed crack in her heart breaking open once more. She was aware her voice sounded as mechanical as the ones heard on automated telephone answering services, but she couldn't help it. "I think that would be very nice."

Sophia must have picked up on a vestige of her pain. "It's just a thought," she said quietly.

"It's a lovely name. It's a lovely idea." Patsy gave her daughter's hand a squeeze. Soon, she promised herself. She'd tell Sophia everything soon, even if she had to do it without Dean's help and support. Another pain scorched the edges of her heart.

"There will be lots of time to pick out baby names if we can't talk Grandpa into coming around soon. I can't imagine being married without the whole family there." She sniffed back a sob.

"Don't cry, Sophia. Milo will come around," Juliana stated flatly. Then she changed the subject. "I hate to be the one to break up this party but I need to get home and get some sleep." She flipped her notebook shut and stuck the pencil in the wire spiral that held the pages together. "I have to start cooking tomorrow. And they're delivering the turkey first thing in the morning, too."

They all took their cue and stood up, Sophia hurrying to the bedroom to get their coats. "I think we have the menu all planned out," Juliana said. She always wanted help planning the menu but she never wanted anyone else to do the cooking. This year Patsy wondered if she shouldn't have been a little more adamant offering to take responsibility for some of the side dishes. Juliana looked tired. Her skin had an alarming gray tint beneath her makeup and she moved slowly as though she might be in some discomfort. Still her eyes were bright and her smile as ready as always. Patsy wondered if she wasn't projecting her own misery onto her husband's grandmother.

"We're just going to be a small group this year," Juliana explained to Alicia, for the third time, as they walked toward the door. "Steve and Heidi will be by in the evening but Larry and Crystal are going to spend the holiday with her parents. Making nice. Building bridges." She rolled her eyes heavenward. Steve was

Dean's nephew and Kent's spotter. Heidi his fiancée. Larry, Dean's older brother, had also fallen in love during the racing season with a much younger woman and her parents were still not completely comfortable with the matchup. "Ordinarily, I would have had him ask them all to the farm for cocktails or something," Juliana continued. "Show Crystal's parents that the May-December thing works fine but I'm so aggravated at that man of mine right now, it would surely not have the effect I was hoping for. Probably break them up on the spot." She giggled a little, obviously feeling the effects of her second glass of wine. "So it will just be the eight of us. Including Sophia and Justin. I don't care what Milo thinks."

Milo, Juliana, Kent and Tanya. Justin and Sophia, herself. And Dean? Dear Lord she hoped he would be there. He wouldn't hurt Juliana that way just to stay away from her, would he?

It was all so complicated now. She was going to have to leave the farm, find a place of her own. There was no other solution. Her spirits dropped even further, leaving a dull ache in the middle of her stomach. That would put even more strain on Juliana managing the big old house and Milo, as well. She would have to help Dean's grandmother find a housekeeper, someone other than the cleaning service that came twice a month to do routine chores. Another change for the older couple that would upset their cherished routines. Guilt gnawed at her.

"Nana—" Sophia protested, holding out Juliana's coat for her to slip into.

Juliana held up a restraining hand. "No buts, Sophia.

You and Justin will be there. One o'clock sharp. Milo will behave himself. It's my house, too, and you are my family." She patted Sophia on the cheek, gold bracelets jingling musically. "My great-grandchild even though we're not connected by blood but by ties of the heart, more powerful still." Her voice broke and she enfolded Sophia in a tight hug. "It will all work out. Have I ever lied to you?"

Sophia's eyes filled with tears. "No, Nana. You've never lied to me. We'll be there. But I'm still afraid—"

"No, you are not," Juliana said sternly. "You are concerned, aggravated, fed-up-to-your-eyeballs with Grosso male bullheadedness. But you are not afraid," she finished with a flourish of her beringed left hand.

"I am all those things," Sophia agreed with a smile—sunshine coming out from behind rain clouds, was the way Dean always described it. "But I am *not* afraid."

"YOU NEED TO TELL her and Kent about Gina," Juliana said, breaking a silence that had lasted since she'd buckled herself into Patsy's car and they pulled out into the street in front of Sophia's apartment to return to the home they shared.

"I know." They had left the lights of Concord behind and were now deep into the North Carolina countryside only a few miles from the home they both loved, and she would soon be leaving.

"It's just so hard to know how to begin. How can I—how can Dean and I—explain to them why we've kept her existence secret for so many years."

"Secrets are terrible things, hard to keep and hurtful when those you kept them from learn about the deception. I know. Milo has secrets, too," Juliana said almost as though she were alone in the car. "Things he has kept hidden inside him for too many years. Nightmares from half a lifetime ago that still keep him awake at night. Secrets kept too long grow septic and fester. They poison everything and we're running out of time to get them out into the open." Her voice broke momentarily. "I'm afraid for his immortal soul."

"What secrets, Juliana?" Patsy asked, disturbed by the anguish in the older woman's voice.

"Nothing, Patsy. Just a tipsy old woman's ramblings," she said, straightening in her seat, brushing a shaking hand over her upswept hair. "Pay me no mind."

"Whatever you wish. But you're right about keeping secrets. Still, it's hard to talk of Gina even after all these years. Do you think Kent and Sophia will understand that and forgive us?"

"They will understand, and you won't need forgiveness, but you dare not put it off much longer." There was an underlying sadness to Juliana's tone that seemed to go even deeper than the old pain of Patsy's lost baby.

"The hits just keep on coming," Patsy said, aware her own voice was thick with unshed tears. "I don't think I should tell them about Gina without Dean. And he won't even return my calls so we're back to square one."

"What happened after you two got back from Florida?" Juliana asked. Patsy sensed Juliana had turned her head to look at her. "Something must have. You seemed on cordial enough terms after the race. Now you're so estranged you aren't even speaking to each other."

"I was stupid," Patsy said bluntly. "Incredibly stupid. And now I've pushed him so far away I don't think I'll ever get him back."

"He agreed to come for Thanksgiving dinner," Juliana said hopefully.

"He did? I wouldn't know. As I said, we haven't spoken for a week."

"He left me a voice mail yesterday. Said he'd be back in town Wednesday afternoon and would be at the farm at one o'clock sharp Thanksgiving Day."

"He's doing that for you and Milo. For our children's sake." She clenched her hands on the steering wheel. He would always be there for the ones he loved, just not for her.

Juliana laid her hand on Patsy's arm. "I'm sorry, Patsy. I wish there was something more I could do. Something I could say to Dean that would help. I'd give my life for all of you." She sounded old and weary and it frightened Patsy.

"I know you would do anything to help, Nana," she said. "But if I'm going to get Dean back I'm going to have to do it on my own."

"You *do* want him back, don't you?"

"More than anything else in the world."

CHAPTER SIXTEEN

"NANA INSISTS we show up for Thanksgiving dinner just as if Grandpa and I hadn't had that awful argument," Sophia said.

She was snuggled against Justin in her bed. They hadn't spent much time at his cabin at Lake Norman, even less at his house in Mooresville where he seldom stayed, himself. It was a long drive for Sophia to make on weekday mornings, and every weekend had been taken up with races during the season.

He'd like to live out at the lake after they were married, though. He'd watched Rachel remodel their parents' house over the past year and it had made him anxious to work on his own place, turn it into a home for the two of them. But before they tackled the cabin he needed to buy that new motor home he'd picked out. They would be spending as much time in it as they would their home in the next couple of years. The Manor had made her last cross-country trip.

Sophia was still talking and he refocused on what she was saying. "I hate being at odds with Grandpa but he's so stubborn and set in his ways." Her breath was warm against his skin. He reached down and put his hand over hers where it rested on his stomach. They had made love and she had responded to him with her usual passion. Afterwards she had not fallen asleep but lay beside him staring into the darkness.

He had pulled her close against him, kissed the top of her head and asked her what was wrong. It hadn't taken more than a moment or two for the words to start tumbling out. "Mom and Nana both looked so sad when they left," she whispered, lifting her head to look up at him. "I don't know what to do for them. I never really believed my parents were actually going to get a divorce, but now I think it might really happen. I just can't imagine them living apart from each other."

Her voice caught on a little sob. He tightened his arms around her. "I thought when your dad won the championship that they'd get back together." A lot of the speculation on pit road and around the garages had echoed his conclusion but he didn't tell Sophia that. She didn't like thinking about her family's problems being the subject of gossip.

"So did I," she said, sniffling. He reached over and plucked a tissue from the box on the bedside stand and handed it to her.

"Here, take this."

"Thanks," she said and blew her nose. Then she scooted up on the pillow until they were side by side. "I don't know if there's anything I can do to talk sense into my mom and dad. They still treat me like a child when it comes to things like this."

"I imagine that's a pretty common reaction for parents." He wasn't comfortable talking about Dean and Patsy's deteriorating marriage. He'd been raised by a single uncle. In the past he hadn't been in a committed relationship long enough to feel he had any expertise in the arena at all. But right now Sophia didn't want expert advice. She wanted a sounding board. Someone to listen to her. Someone she could bounce ideas off of. He could handle that. Just as long as she didn't start crying again.

"I suppose it is. But she's always been able to talk to Nana. Except for tonight Nana seemed as off balance and upset about her problems with Grandpa as Mom." She laid her head on his chest again. "I just can't believe this is happening to my family. And now when Dad's finally won the championship and we should all be happy as clams." She fell silent for a moment and he hoped she had fallen asleep. She hadn't, he realized when she started talking again. "Even if Mom and Dad come to their senses and get back together there's still Grandpa to worry about."

"Sophia, we might have to accept the fact that Milo is never going to get used to having me around. I can live with it. I just wish you could."

Once more she bounced upright, rolling halfway over him so that their faces were mere inches apart. He would only have to tip his head a little to bring their lips together, but he didn't move a muscle. She wasn't in the mood for lovemaking. She was in the mood for talking. And more than just talking, he suspected, making plans.

"I do not want to hear you say that ever again," Sophia commanded, her eyes shimmering blue fire even in the near darkness of her bedroom. "You are the man I love and you're going to be my husband. You're going to be part of the family."

"A hardscrabble Murphy amongst the almighty Grossos?" He snorted back a laugh.

"Yes, the almighty Grossos," she repeated. "Grandpa would see reason if we could just find who was driving the truck the night your father was killed, clear away those old rumors that it was a member of my family even though my dad had a solid alibi. I know it's upsetting for you, but don't you think we owe it to ourselves to try and settle this once and for all? I'll start searching the Internet. All we need is a lead of some kind to get started. I'll do it now. Tonight. I know I've talked about it off and on all summer but it's time to stop talking and take some action." She made as if to get out of bed and Justin reached out, encircling her with his arms, preventing her from leaving his side.

"It's not that simple, Sophia," he said, choosing his words with great care. "It's a cold case. The files are sealed. The news reports were sketchy and full of all kinds of wild speculation."

"I know it's going to take more than a couple hours of searching the Web for old racing articles and police reports," she said, sounding every bit as stubborn as her great-grandfather. "But it *is* a start. Maybe I can come up with something to show Grandpa by Thanksgiving. A peace offering," she said almost wistfully.

Justin's gut twisted. She was hurting. She loved Milo and Juliana and being estranged from the old man was almost as upsetting to her as her parents' foundering marriage. "Sophia, lie still. It's late. You'll only exhaust yourself tonight." He had never felt so conflicted in his life, caught between his promise to the man who had raised him as his own son and the woman he loved.

"I won't get any more rest if I stay in bed. I can't sleep. I just keep thinking something might happen to Grandpa before I can make things right with him." But she didn't make any further attempt to get out of bed. They lay silently wrapped in each other's arms for a few minutes. He closed his eyes and tried to take his own advice and sleep, but his roiling thoughts wouldn't let him rest.

Sophia had relaxed against him again but he knew from her breathing that she wasn't asleep, either. A few moments later he felt the wetness of her tears on his chest and then a muffled sob that almost broke his heart. "Sophia, don't cry," he said. "Please."

"I can't help it. The holidays are coming. They're my favorite time of the year. Dad and Kent are home. We're all together, not flying off here and there to one race track or another. It's always been our family time. And now look at us. Everything's a mess. Everyone's walking on eggshells and my parents are living in different zip codes. I hate it." She started crying harder. "I'm sorry," she sniffed as he reached out for another tissue. "But you already know you're marrying a crybaby." A hiccupping little sob escaped her lips. She tried to turn it into a giggle but it didn't quite work.

Justin felt his heart twist painfully. His loyalty now belonged to this woman he loved so completely. Surely, Hugo would release him from his promise if he were here. He wasn't though. He and Sylvie had taken a few days away together and not disclosed their destination. Justin suspected they had eloped. He made his decision. His word was not so important to him, as what he felt for the woman beside him. He reached down and lifted Sophia's chin with the tip of his finger. He kissed her lightly. "I know how my father died, Sophia. I've known for several weeks now," he said quietly.

She lay very still, her hand on his heart. For a moment she didn't speak. "Justin, how did you find this out? Who told you?" He could hear the fear in her voice. She still couldn't be certain that it wasn't a member of her immediate family who had run his father down and left him for dead so long ago. She was trembling. He closed his hand over hers.

"It wasn't any of your kin, Sophia," he said, finding it harder to tell the old, sad story than he had thought it would be. It was his father he was talking about, after all, a man he'd never known, figured he probably wouldn't have liked all that much if he had, but his father, nonetheless. "It was Sylvie."

"Kim's birth mother?" Disbelief echoed through her words. "I don't understand. She could hardly have known him. Why would she have wanted to kill him? Was it an accident?" She raised herself on her elbow stared down at him, a myriad of questions swirling in her eyes.

"She knew him well enough to be afraid of him. Deathly afraid of him," he said, his voice rough with the residue of old hurt and abandonment he'd thought he'd put aside in recent months. "He was stalking her and coming on to her. She just couldn't take it anymore, I guess."

"I see," she said softly. "Poor Sylvie. But why didn't she go to the police? Or to Hugo? He would have protected her. He wouldn't stand for anything like that."

"He never knew," Justin said, doing his best to sort out all the tangled elements of the decades-old tragedy. "I only found this out myself. She had been abused before when she was only fourteen and was afraid of it happening again."

"Oh, God. Is that how she got pregnant with Kim?" she said making her own deductions.

He nodded, realized she couldn't see him, and said, "Yes. She was just getting her life back together when she met and married Hugo. When my dad started in on her, too, she just couldn't handle it. She was afraid Hugo wouldn't take her word against his brother's, that he'd throw her and Kim out into the street."

"Oh, Justin." She curled herself tightly against him. "How alone she must have felt. How frightened she must have been."

"Yeah. Young. No money. No education to speak of. She didn't know where to turn and then—" He stopped for a moment, swallowed hard. God, he didn't want to confess what happened next to Sophia. He loved her. He wanted her to be the mother of his children, but he was afraid when she learned everything about the night Troy Murphy died she would never, ever quite trust him again.

"Go on, Justin. Tell me what happened the night your dad died?"

"He threatened her. And Kim. Threatened to hurt them both, if she ever went to the police or to my uncle and told them what he'd tried to do. She believed him," he said bitterly.

"Your mother suffered from postpartum depression, you told me, remember?" Sophia reminded him gently.

"And my father's lousy treatment of her didn't help the situation."

"But Sylvie didn't deliberately run him down, did she?" Sophia asked.

"No. She only meant to frighten him but he stepped the wrong way and she felt a thump. She thought he had punched her fender in anger. She didn't see him in her rearview mirror, so she drove off. It wasn't until the police showed up to inform them of his death that she realized she had killed him."

"Then Hugo took you and Rachel to raise as his own even though they were both just kids yet themselves. It must have been a nightmare for her seeing your sad little faces every day, knowing she'd killed your father and made you orphans."

"Yeah. It was too much for her. She just up and left."

"And left her own baby behind. Knowing she'd never see Kim again." He could feel her crying again, tears of sorrow and empathy for a woman she barely knew. "All those lost years. Her punishment was far worse than anything a judge and jury could have meted out."

"You're right there. Hugo and Sylvie consulted a lawyer. He said there's not enough evidence to file charges against her. I think he figured the same thing you did. She'd been punished enough," he said bitterly.

"Oh, Justin." She wrapped her arms around his neck, kissed him over and over, soothingly, lovingly, and he felt a little of the icy chill that had been seeping through his skin into his bones melt away at the touch of her lips and the salty warmth of her tears. "I'm so sorry. So very sorry. But you're not your father, remember that.

I've told you before and I believe what I said with all my heart. You didn't inherit his bad traits. You have to believe it, too."

He kissed her back, wanting nothing more than to stop all this talk of death and betrayal and make love to her. "When I'm with you I do believe it. That's why I want us to get married. To be together every day for the rest of our lives."

"I want that, too. And we will be soon."

"Will you forgive me for keeping this to myself? I gave Hugo my word."

"I'm disappointed you didn't tell me sooner, that you carried the burden of it all alone. I can be trusted with your secrets," she admonished, then relented with her next words. "But you gave your word. I know how important that is, even if it's not logical."

"It won't happen again," he said and he meant it. They were a team now, partners. Partners didn't keep secrets from each other.

"I know it won't happen again." She spoke his thoughts aloud as though she'd plucked them out of his brain. "We're partners now. A team. That means no secrets."

"No secrets."

"My parents deserve to know the truth," she said. He could feel her staring into the darkness above their heads.

"Sylvie agrees but Hugo thinks she needs more time to regain her strength."

"I can understand that. She's been through a lot but I couldn't keep a secret like this from them for any length of time. You understand that, don't you?"

"Soon, Sophia. We'll tell them soon." She was quiet then but he could still feel tension strumming through her body. "Your mind's still going a mile a minute."

"It's a lot to absorb. And there's still your great-uncle Connor," she said softly. "I'm not so certain that no kin of mine was involved in his death. I think the rumors that Dad might have had something to do with your father's death got started because of the older one still floating around out there."

"You mean that Milo might have been driving the truck that forced Connor's motorcycle off the road?"

"Yes," she said. She shivered a little and wrapped her arms around his neck. "I'm afraid the truth of what happened to him that night will still come back to haunt us all one day."

CHAPTER SEVENTEEN

THANKSGIVING WAS Dean's favorite holiday. It meant the NASCAR season was over. He wouldn't be traveling—at least not as much. He and Patsy would have time for themselves, Champions Week in New York the years he made the Chase for the NASCAR Sprint Cup, shows and shopping and museums and art galleries for Patsy and Juliana and Sophia. Too many TV appearances for him, and meet-and-greets, but he always got a kick out of wheeling his car around Times Square. Then a little down time; Christmas at the farm, New Year's Eve with friends, a week on a beach somewhere before it all started up again with winter testing and Speedweeks at Daytona. Time to get back in the car. Time to race.

Except next year he wouldn't be driving the car. The thought always caught him off guard no matter how many times a day it crossed his mind.

What would he be doing from now on? Sitting behind Alan's desk, trying to decide if they needed one more session in the wind tunnel? Whether or not to build their own engines or do a deal with one of the bigger teams with their stable of hotshot engineers and designers? How was the best way to bring along the younger drivers, keep them in the NASCAR Craftsman Truck Series another season or move them up to the NASCAR Nationwide Series? All his decisions to make. If the deal to buy the remaining shares of Cargill Motors didn't fall through completely. And if the takeover did come to be, would he would be making those decisions with a woman who was no longer his wife? How could they be successful partners in a business venture when they couldn't be partners in their private life?

On the other hand what would he do with himself if he didn't buy his old race team? That possibility brought him awake in the middle of the night more and more often these days. He could probably go into broadcasting. He wasn't that bad looking. He had most of his hair, and he could string a dozen sentences together without embarrassing himself. But show business didn't appeal to him. Neither did the rubber-chicken motivational-speaking gigs, or the charity golf tournament circuit that occupied some of the other retired drivers.

He didn't have a second career to fall back on. He'd been a race car driver all his adult life. It's all he knew. It's all he wanted to know. He had a couple of seasons in him yet. If everything else in his life fell apart he could get a ride somewhere.

But he'd given Patsy his word. He intended to honor it.

He was retired.

And unemployed. And on the fast track to being divorced from the woman he loved. How the hell did that happen?

He caught a glimpse of his scowling face in the

rearview mirror of his truck and made an effort to get rid of the frown. He had one more chance today. If he could get Patsy alone somewhere in that big old house and apologize, ask her to forgive him for running out on her, maybe they could patch things up. Start over again, just the two of them the way it had been when they were young.

He could do it. He knew Patsy loved him, too; she'd said so. But she was afraid now of the future, and to tell the truth, so was he a little. Time had a way of doing that to a man. But he wasn't about to give up, roll over and call it quits just yet. He was going to win her back. There was no other acceptable outcome.

He climbed out of the truck and grabbed the two bottles of wine that Juliana had told him he could bring to contribute to the huge dinner she was cooking. He wasn't a big wine drinker so he'd let the guy at the wine shop pick them out. One was white; the other red. One from California. One from Australia.

Patsy had always wanted to go to Australia but they'd never found the time. There were a lot of race fans in Oz though. He'd like to make the trip. Maybe this would be the year. If he could win her back.

Always that caveat. Always that condition to his every plan. He slammed the door of his truck and started walking. He glanced around the yard, taking a moment to watch Milo's beloved quarter horses grazing in the still green pasture beyond the fence. He'd always pictured himself growing old with the same view. He wondered if he would live as long as his grandfather. Forty more years if he were that lucky. Unthinkable to spend them without his Patsy-girl.

A dark blue 4x4 was parked beside Kent's truck in front of one of the garage bays. Justin and Sophia, he surmised. The boy had guts showing up in direct defiance of Milo's ultimatum. Dean wondered if they'd get through the day without the old man blowing off a head of steam. If Milo did disrupt the celebration he'd have to step in and take him in hand. He seldom crossed his grandfather, even when he was at his most cantankerous, because he loved and respected the old man. But if crossing swords with Milo meant Sophia's future happiness then he would do what needed to be done.

"Dean! You're finally here. I was just about to send a posse out after you," Juliana called from behind the big island where she was making last-minute adjustments to a number of side dishes and relishes. "Come, have a bite of my antipasto. There's still a few nibbles left."

His stomach growled as he hung his jacket beside all the others on the brass hooks on the utility porch, retrieved his wine from the top of the washing machine and stepped into the kitchen. His mouth watered as his senses were bombarded with dozens of aromas and good smells. The turkey was already out of the oven, resting under a tent of aluminum foil, waiting for his skills as chief carver. He knew the skin would be golden brown and crispy and the meat beneath so moist and tender it almost melted in your mouth.

Patsy was working at the stove, whipping a large crockery bowl of potatoes with a stick blender while Tanya garnished Juliana's famous sweet potato casserole with handfuls of tiny marshmallows. His wife pretended not to see him and he returned the gesture. "What shall I do with the wine, Nana?" he asked to cover the awkward moment.

"Kent. Come open the wine for your father. The red should breathe a little before we eat. And you can top off my glass while you're at it." She indicated a half-full glass of red wine at her elbow.

"Yes, ma'am," Kent responded with a jaunty salute. "Just as soon as they finish this set of downs. Looks like Carolina might score."

"That will take at least ten minutes," Juliana grumbled under her breath taking a wine bottle from the counter and topping off her glass, herself. "Just like when they say two minutes left in the half. That's such a joke."

"Hi, Dad." Sophia hovered protectively by Justin's side as they cleaned and arranged a platter of raw vegetables, crudités, they called them on the cooking channel. He'd been watching a lot of late night TV this last week, sleepless in his tiny borrowed apartment near the garage. His daughter was smiling but her body language was tense and anxious.

"Hi, honey," he said, smiling back, pretending all was right with the world.

"Good afternoon, sir," Justin said, obviously on his best behavior. "Happy Thanksgiving."

"Same to you. Good to see you." Dean moved across the room to offer his hand. "Smells great in here, doesn't it?"

"Like Heaven," Justin agreed.

Dean plucked a cherry tomato from the tray they were arranging and popped it in his mouth. Sophia set down her knife and wiped her hands on the vintage feed sack apron she had tied around her waist and opened her arms for a hug. "How's it going, baby?" he whispered in her ear.

"Okay, I guess," she whispered back. "Grandpa's ignoring us for the most part but he did say hello to Justin when we got here. I think that's a hopeful sign, don't you?"

Dean glanced in his grandfather's direction. Milo and Kent were seated in front of the big-screen TV watching football. It was Detroit playing Carolina. Later in the afternoon Dallas would play New Orleans. Earlier Milo would have watched the Macy's Thanksgiving Day parade. His grandfather had a soft spot for the big balloons, although he would have denied it with his last breath.

"It beats a fist in the eye," Dean whispered back, hoping to tease Sophia into a more genuine smile.

"That's what I told her," Justin said as he picked up the plate of vegetables and looked around for a place to set them on the already crowded countertop of the island, where Juliana was now inventorying an array of desserts.

"It's not funny, you two," Sophia scolded under her breath, but a few of the shadows had receded from her eyes when she realized that Dean was now firmly on the young couple's side of the family divide.

"Hello, Dean," Tanya said. "Want to inspect my handiwork?" She gestured to the bowl of sweet potatoes. "Does this pass muster?"

"Looks great to me," he said, wondering if he should offer her a hug. Kent's fiancée was not an effusive person. Calm and composed, she seldom made extravagant emotional gestures of any kind. He settled for a nod and a pat on the shoulder. "Can't wait to give them a try."

"Thank you, kind sir," Tanya said. "Now, shoo. Out of my way. These need to go on the table."

"Dad, can I pour you a glass of wine?" Kent asked.

"I'd rather have a beer."

"We can manage that," Kent responded, heading for the utility room where a second refrigerator held drinks and, more than likely, still more food destined for the over-laden table.

"Dean, we've been waiting for you to carve the turkey," Juliana reminded him as he accepted the cold beer from his son with a nod of thanks. She filled a bowl with steamed fresh vegetables that had in recent years taken the place of the more traditional green bean casserole, which Dean secretly preferred, then partially redeemed herself by topping them with a generous pat of real butter.

"I'm at your disposal," he said. She was dressed in a long denim skirt and tunic-like blouse splashed with large multicolored flowers. There were dark circles under her eyes and her skin had a sallow look to it that gave him pause. Was she ill, or was it that the flowered blouse just wasn't a good choice for her skin tones?

Jeez, he thought. *Listen to me.* Where had that come from? All those middle-of-the-night infomercials for skin products probably.

"Are you all right, Nana?" he asked, bending to give her a peck on the cheek. "You look tired."

"I am tired," she said tartly. "And it's ungentlemanly of you to say so to a lady, you know."

"Not if you care about that lady's well-being," he said, ratcheting up his drawl. "Then it's considerate."

"In that case you're forgiven. To tell you the truth," she said, never taking her eyes from the fruit she was arranging in an antique cut-crystal dish, "I am feeling a little under the weather right now. But it's probably just indigestion. I'll be fine once we are all at table together. Go. Pay Milo some attention and then be ready to carve in exactly two minutes. Everything will be ready by then."

"Yes, ma'am." He took a step away from the island and came face-to-face with Patsy, who was holding the huge bowl of golden mashed potatoes in both hands.

"Hello, Dean," she said.

"Hello, Patsy." His throat was dry as a bone all of a sudden. She looked beautiful, her skin still retaining just a hint of golden tan, her hair all sleek and shining against her cheeks. She was wearing slim black slacks and a ruby-red sweater set. As always she wore the tiny golden cross around her throat. She had taken off her wedding ring, but not the necklace he had given her to remember Gina by.

They stood there, each not quite meeting the other's gaze head on. "If you'll excuse me, I'll set this on the table."

"What? Sure. Out of the way," he said, his voice cracking as though he were fourteen again. He held up his hands and took a step sideways, then made a beeline for Milo's end of the room as though he were heading for the checkered flag at Daytona.

"Hey, Milo. What's the score?" he asked, leaning over the back of Milo's big recliner. The back of his neck tingled and he wondered if Patsy was watching him. He stayed where he was, didn't dare turn his head and look over his shoulder. He wasn't certain what would be worse. That she was watching him with that cool, distant expression on her face. Or that she had gone on about her business as though he didn't even exist.

On second thought this was worse than being fourteen again.

"I could use a beer," Milo grumbled from the depths of his chair, nodding toward the brown bottle in Dean's hand. He looked like a wizened old gnome sitting on a throne of leather and brass studs.

"Sure thing," Dean said, glad for something to do to take his mind off his wife.

"You don't need a beer, Milo," Juliana said with an edge to her voice.

"That woman has ears like a bat," Dean said under his breath to Kent, not sure exactly what to do next. At any other time he would shoot Patsy a glance and she would come to his rescue. She always knew the right thing to say, the right moves to make in a situation like this one. But Patsy wasn't going to help him out this time. He was on his own.

"We're just about ready to sit down to table. How about I pour you a glass of wine instead?" he suggested to his grandfather.

Milo raised himself from the confines of the big chair, uncoiling slowly, his arthritic limbs protesting audibly. "I said I want a beer. That's what I meant."

Juliana whirled from her command center at the island, gold bracelets jingling irritably, and put her hands on her hips. "And I said you don't need a beer. We are going to eat in less than ten minutes. Dean, if you will be so kind as to start carving the bird."

"I'm eating here. On my TV tray," Milo said, his mouth set in a grim line. He narrowed his eyes and waited, daring Juliana to contradict him again. He rested both hands on the top of his cane and locked gazes with his wife. "And I want a beer with my meal."

"You will sit at the table with your family," she said. "Or I will walk out of this kitchen and never speak a word to you again."

"Nana." Patsy set the bowl of potatoes on the Irish lace tablecloth that had been a wedding gift to Milo and his first wife, Frances, Dean's grandmother, and walked over to Juliana, the grandmother of his heart. She put her hand on the older woman's arm. "It's nothing so terrible if Milo wants a beer with his dinner," she said softly.

"It is," Juliana said, her voice tight with strain. "He's not supposed to drink beer. It upsets his stomach and aggravates his gout. He knows that. He's just being stubborn and bullheaded and I am simply fed up with it."

"I'm being bullheaded? What about you? Insisting I have a devil's spawn of a Murphy under my roof. At my table. Eating my food and making plans to carry off my Sophia? You're lucky I didn't slam the door in his face or better yet fill his rear end full of birdshot."

"Grandpa," Sophia whispered. "Please. We've been getting along so well this morning."

"Hah," Milo snorted. "I've been tolerating him for your sake, that's all."

Dean decided it was time to intervene. He couldn't let Patsy handle this all on her own. Sophia was too upset by Milo's renewed criticism of Justin, and Kent and Tanya seemed paralyzed by the unusual sight of Milo and Juliana quarreling in public. "Milo. Nana. Let's all sit down. It's Thanksgiving. Milo, if you want to drink a beer and suffer the consequences with your stomach or trigger an attack of gout, so be it. As far as I know you've still got your right mind and it's up to you if you want to make yourself miserable."

"I've got my right mind. I'm not sure about some of the others in this room, though," Milo mumbled under his breath, beginning to look—and Dean suspected, feel—a bit sheepish.

"Are you okay with that, Nana?" he asked, switching his gaze to Milo's wife.

"Fine," she said, wringing a dishcloth between her hands. "Fine. Whatever he wants. As long as we can eat in peace. I've been cooking for two days. I don't want it all to go to waste."

"I'm not planning on letting that happen," Kent said heartily, coming forward to take the turkey on its china platter from the counter to its place of honor at the head of the table. "I've had my eye on the drumstick since the moment I got here."

"Milo," Tanya said, taking her cue from Kent, "will you walk with me to my chair?" she asked.

"I'd be delighted." He lifted his head and straightened his shoulders as he held out his arm in a gallant gesture from days gone by.

"Nana," Dean said following his grandfather's lead, "may I escort you to your seat?"

She stood where she was, her hands clutched beneath her chest, her face suddenly drained of all color. "No," she whispered in a strangled voice. "I think you should call nine-one-one instead. I think I might be having a heart attack."

CHAPTER EIGHTEEN

FOR A MOMENT Patsy didn't think she had heard correctly. Juliana? A heart attack? Her grandmother-in-law was one of the strongest women Patsy knew. She was never ill. Never caught the flu. Seldom even had the sniffles. How could she be having a heart attack when only five minutes earlier she had been ordering them all around like a general on maneuvers?

But something was definitely wrong with Juliana. Dean had both arms around her shoulders leading her to a seat in Milo's big chair. Her face was deathly pale. She was sweating and trembling. Milo was leaning over the back of the chair, smoothing her hair, his own face as white as hers. "Juliana, my love. What's wrong? What's wrong?" he repeated, his voice filled with concern.

"Pain. Pain in my chest. In my back. Everywhere," Juliana gasped.

Milo looked at Dean, then at Patsy. "Do something," he begged. "Hurry."

"I'll make the call," Tanya said, calm and controlled as always, as she reached for the handset of the kitchen phone.

"Nana…" Sophia dropped to her knees beside the

chair, reaching out to gently tug Juliana's wrist onto the padded arm so that she could take her pulse.

"Am I dying?" Juliana gasped. "It feels like it." Her fist was still pressed against her breast.

"Can you describe the pain?" Sophia asked. She was in full head-nurse mode now, focused completely on her patient. Patsy was just grateful that there was no blood involved. Sophia had an alarming tendency to faint at the sight of blood, the main reason she'd chosen to become a nursing administrator.

"It's everywhere," Juliana gasped. "Across my back. Up my neck." She was fighting for breath, her face pale her skin tone a mottled gray.

"Juliana, my love." Milo stroked her hair with a shaking hand. "Please, no more talking. Save your breath."

She nodded, tilting her head to rest her cheek against his hand. "I am, Milo. I'm trying."

Tanya, who had been speaking with the 911 dispatcher now hung up the phone and joined them.

"How long?" Dean asked her.

Patsy had dropped to her knees on Juliana's other side. "The closest EMT unit is already out on a run. It will be twenty minutes before they can get another one here," Tanya disclosed. The local emergency unit relied on volunteers and when they were out of service, as was evidently the case now, help had to come from much farther away.

Patsy glanced at Dean, she couldn't stop herself. He had been her rock for more than thirty years. It was a hard habit to break not to look to him for solace and guidance when there was an emergency. "Twenty minutes. That seems like a long time to wait."

"It is," Sophia agreed. "But I don't see what else we can do."

"We can drive her into Concord ourselves," Dean said with his usual quiet self-confidence. "We'll call ahead to the hospital and tell them we're coming. We can be there in less than twenty minutes."

He glanced at Kent, who nodded slightly. "A lot less than twenty minutes."

"Can you hold on that long, my love?" Milo asked, his voice filled with anxiety.

"If I have to," Juliana said weakly.

"Kent, Justin. Make a cradle of your arms," Sophia directed, rising to her feet. She smiled down at her great-grandmother. "Nana, they're going to carry you down the steps to the car just the way you and Grandpa used to carry me over big mud puddles when I was little."

"I'd prefer to walk," Juliana murmured.

"You'll do as you're told," Milo commanded with such authority that everyone turned their head in his direction, amazed at the power in his usually feeble voice. "Do you hear me, Juliana?"

"Yes, Milo," Juliana said, a faint hint of color seeping back into her face, a slight smile on her lips. "I'll go quietly, but hurry please. I hurt so badly."

"I'll bring the truck to the door," Tanya offered. "Nana can stretch out in the backseat. It will be more comfortable for her."

"Good idea."

"You'll need your coat. It's cold outside." Patsy rose and hurried to fetch Juliana's coat. The sky had clouded over an hour or so earlier and it was beginning to rain. She knew better than to suggest they wrap her in a blanket. Juliana would never hear of such an indignity.

"And my purse, Patsy. Don't forget my purse," the older woman commanded, standing with help from Dean and Sophia. "My health card. My driver's license. We'll need them for the insurance."

"I'll take care of all the paperwork, Juliana. You just stay calm." Milo moved spryly toward the kitchen door.

Juliana turned, Dean and Sophia on either side and moaned aloud.

"Nana, is the pain worse?" Sophia asked sharply. Patsy's heart rate spiked with alarm as she held Juliana's coat for her to slip into.

Juliana shook her head. "No. But my food. All my lovely food. It will all have to be thrown away." She looked as if she might start to cry.

Tanya had returned in time to hear the last remark. She looked over at Kent and he nodded. "Nana, Kent and I will stay behind and take care of the food so it doesn't spoil."

"Right," Kent said. "We'll get it all covered and into the fridge. Everything will be waiting when we get back from the hospital."

"We'll be as quick as we can. We'll meet up with you at the hospital. How does that sound, Nana?"

"Thank you, Tanya. That will ease my mind."

"We won't be more than a few minutes behind you," Kent assured them. He gestured toward his great-grandmother with his left hand and Justin stepped forward. "Ready, Nana?"

"Oh, dear," she said, settling into the cradle formed by their linked arms. "I'm too heavy for you."

"No, you're not," Kent said. "We're stock car drivers remember. Lots of upper body strength."

"He's right," Justin agreed, but he sounded a bit breathless nonetheless.

"Be careful. Watch the steps," Sophia directed as Patsy held open the door to the utility porch and then hurried to do the same with the door to the outside of the house.

"Milo and I, Nana and Sophia will go in the truck," Dean instructed, taking the keys from Tanya. "Justin, you and Patsy follow us in your truck?"

"Yes, sir."

Patsy felt a twinge of dismay and hurt feelings that she was being excluded from Juliana's presence. She wondered if it was because Dean didn't even want to be in the same car with her, but she shrugged off the unworthy thought. Sophia was the medical professional. She needed to be with Juliana and Milo was not to be separated from his wife even for a moment. It would crowd them all to have another person in the SUV. She would get there just as quickly riding with Justin. Juliana let out a low, stifled moan and, ashamed, Patsy jerked her thoughts away from her own misery. "It won't be long now, Nana," she said soothingly. "We will be right behind you."

Juliana, looking exhausted, only nodded. "Please hurry. The pain is getting worse."

CHAPTER NINETEEN

"HOW FAST IS Dean driving?" Patsy asked Justin. She was sitting beside him in the front seat, her hands wrapped so tightly around the strap of her shoulder bag she could feel her fingernails biting into her skin.

"A few miles over the speed limit," Justin said with a grim smile.

Patsy glanced over at the speedometer. "More than a few," she said. "I wish we could go faster. I never realized it could seem to take so long to drive twelve miles." She was talking to keep her teeth from chattering with nerves and fear.

"Feels like we're standing still," he admitted. "But the roads out here aren't in the best of shape. The rough ride would be hard on Juliana." They bounced over a washboard patch left by the last big rain, adding emphasis to his words.

"It still feels as if we're just crawling along," Patsy said, clutching her bag tight against her side, as though doing so would help hold in her terror.

"We'll be there in five minutes," Justin said, tapping the brake to slow their speed as they came into busier traffic.

"I hope they have someone waiting for us at the emergency entrance."

"I'm sure they will," he said. "Sophia's alerted them that we're coming. I can see her on her cell phone now." Patsy couldn't see any such thing but she didn't doubt he did. Many stock car drivers had exceptional long-range vision and depth perception. "Once they know it's Juliana Grosso who's the patient they'll be there with bells on."

Patsy shot him a glance. He hadn't quite been able to filter all the bitterness from his voice.

He looked over at her for a brief second. "Sorry," he apologized. "I didn't mean that the way it sounded."

"I know what you meant," Patsy said. "The Grosso name does open doors in this county."

"A hell of a lot more places than Cabarrus County," Justin said grimly.

"You and Sophia can't seem to catch a break."

"Not with the Grosso patriarch, that's for sure."

"Actually, I was beginning to hope Milo was coming around. After all you'd been in the house for over an hour and he hadn't threatened to throw you out on your backside more than once or twice." She smiled to show him she was making a joke.

"Yeah. We were practically bosom buddies there before Juliana got sick. I was planning to eat myself into a coma to get on her good side."

"You are on her good side," Patsy said. "And mine."

He cleared his throat. "Thanks. I appreciate that. I sure hope Juliana's okay."

"So do I."

"If there isn't a medic waiting at the door, I'll go in there and grab the first doctor I see and drag him back by the scruff of his neck," he offered with a smile of his own.

"I'll help you," she said.

It turned out no such action was necessary. A doctor and two nurses waited at the entrance to the emergency room. They wheeled out a gurney and loaded Juliana onto it with a minimum of delay. By the time Justin and Patsy found a parking space and entered the imposing red brick building, Juliana had already disappeared into an exam room and Milo was perched on the edge of a chair at the admitting counter. Sophia was standing protectively beside him with her hand on his narrow shoulder while a pleasant-faced, middle-aged woman took the insurance information and assured him patiently that he could see Juliana just as soon as the doctors were done examining her.

Patsy looked around the waiting area for Dean but he was nowhere to be seen. Force of habit, she told herself, but knew she was lying. It wasn't force of habit it was the call of her heart. Justin figured out what she was doing and said, "He's parking the truck. They won't let you stay parked outside the doors. Might block an ambulance, ya know."

"Of course. I should have thought of that." She felt her face color. Was she so obvious? She supposed she was. She needed Dean beside her so that she could draw courage from his quiet, steady strength so badly she ached with it.

"Can I get you a cup of coffee or something?" Justin asked solicitously, but it was obvious his attention was focused on Sophia and not Patsy.

"No. Nothing, thanks. I'll just wait here for Dean."

Justin gave her a quick assessing glance and then nodded his agreement. "I guess I'll stay here, too. I don't want to upset Milo any more than he already is." He cut another quick glance in Sophia's direction and then settled onto one of the waiting room chairs.

Too restless to sit, Patsy took a step toward Sophia and Milo but just as she did so the old man rose from his chair, leaning heavily on Sophia's arm and began walking in her direction. "It won't be long now until they let us see her, Grandpa," Sophia said bracingly. "Someone will come to talk to us as soon as they have some idea of what her condition is."

"I want to see her now," he said, sounding every day of his ninety-two years. "I never got to say I was sorry for being such a jackass this past week. I'll never forgive myself if something happens to her." He lifted a shaking hand to his eyes, covering his face to hide his emotions.

"Here, sir. Take my chair," Justin said, surging to his feet. "I'll go find you a cup of tea or would coffee be better?"

Milo stayed where he was, looking at Justin as if he was seeing him for the first time. "I don't want anything to drink, but thank you for offering," he said stiffly then added, "You don't have much of the look of your father about you?" He made it a question, an opening. Patsy held her breath hoping Justin would take his cue.

"No, sir," Justin said. Sophia didn't leave her great-grandfather's side but Patsy could see her tense, anticipating yet another confrontation between the two men. "I've been told I look like my mother," Justin said carefully.

"Blood doesn't always tell, Sophia says."

"I've heard the same opinion from her myself."

"I knew your mother," the elderly man revealed, his faded brown eyes looking inward to the past. "Not well, but I met her once or twice. She was a pretty girl. Quiet and sad. Your father treated her badly."

"I know, sir." Justin had relaxed his stance slightly. His expression was still guarded but his tone was gentle. "He didn't treat her as he should have, but my uncle says he loved her in his way."

"That's no excuse," Milo retorted, his voice gaining strength. "No excuse whatsoever."

"I agree," Justin said, looking him straight in the eye.

"Do you intend to honor and respect my Sophia as she should be honored and respected?"

"Yes, sir," Justin said as solemnly as if he stood before the preacher in church. He looked at Sophia. "I intend to honor her and love her until I draw my last breath on this earth. And maybe beyond that," he added quietly.

Patsy heard the swish of the automatic doors behind her, a waft of cold air across her legs, and then a prickling sense of awareness as she felt Dean come to stand behind her. Sophia looked across the room at her father and smiled. Justin paid Dean no heed, his attention was focused on Milo and Sophia, standing at the old man's side.

Patsy found herself distracted by the warmth of Dean's body close behind her and she wanted nothing more on earth than to be able to lean back and be enclosed in his embrace. He was close, but only in the physical sense. Emotionally he might have been a thousand miles away. Her breath caught in her throat. What had she done over these past months? How could she have believed for a moment it would be better to face the future alone than learn to cope with her fear of losing him? What could she do to make it all right again? To win him back? She was afraid it was too late to even try. Acutely aware of every breath he took, of every beat of his pulse, Patsy did her best to ignore Dean's nearness and focus on what was happening between Justin and Milo. There were tears in Sophia's eyes, but pride, too, in the way Justin was handling the old man's interrogation.

"I've lost a lot in my life, Justin Murphy. My wife. My son and daughter-in-law. My—" He broke off, swallowing hard. "So many dear to me."

Gina, Patsy thought. The old man was thinking of Gina. Once more conscience assailed her. *No more secrets,* she pledged to herself, *no more secrets.*

"I won't take Sophia away from you, sir. She loves all of you too much. She would never be happy away from you."

"She's our world," Milo said simply, his voice rough with emotion. He continued to take Justin's measure, his gaze unwavering. Justin met the scrutiny with quiet dignity. "But what about you? Can you and yours? Can you put your father's death out of your mind and your thoughts? What if someday you start to blame Sophia for an accident that had nothing to do with her? You'll break her heart."

Justin and Sophia exchanged a look. Sophia raised her hand in a pleading gesture. Their eyes held for a long moment then Justin nodded. "I am my father's son, Mr. Grosso," he said. "I won't deny my kin. I doubt you really expect me to. But I've learned some things in the last few weeks. Things that have answered a lot of questions about the night my father died. I'm not free to give you the details just yet, but I can tell you I know a Grosso didn't kill my father."

Milo's head came up. Behind her, Patsy felt Dean stiffen, grow very still. She balled her hand into a fist to keep from reaching out to him. Justin knew who had killed his father? Who? Why? Her mind took off in a dozen directions at once. She could feel the tension radiating from Dean, knew his thoughts paralleled her own. After all these years he would be free of the cloud of suspicion that had hung over them for so long.

"You're telling me the truth? You know who ran down your father that night?" Milo asked, casting his gaze over the few other people in the waiting room, but they seemed to be absorbed in their own problems and beyond a few covert glances at Dean and Justin, they didn't appear to be paying attention to the conversation.

"I do."

"But you won't tell me?"

"I gave my word," Justin said, simply. "Until I'm released from that bond I intend to honor it."

"I can understand that."

"I'll tell you the whole story of what happened that night as soon as I can. You have my word on that, too."

Milo took a deep breath, let it out, almost a sigh. "A man's word should mean something," he said. "But it doesn't change the fact that your father was a bad man. Same with your great-uncle Connor. They were cut from the same cloth. They had no respect for women.

They bullied and abused them. They had no respect for other men's vows. Other men's wives. Or their own. I can't and won't hold with that kind of behavior."

"I promise you I'm not like that. I share a bloodline with them, that's all. But I was raised by a different kind of Murphy. I like to think I take more after him. I've made some mistakes in my past but I've never harmed a woman, or a weaker man. I never will."

"Justin treats me exactly as I want to be treated, Grandpa," Sophia said, her eyes shining with love. "As an equal. We're partners. We each have our own strengths and our own weaknesses to bring to our life together. I love him. He's a good man. I know because growing up with you and Dad in my life has shown me what good men are. I love Justin. He's the man I want to spend the rest of my life with. Please, Grandpa, be happy for me. For us."

"This girl is my world," Milo repeated more strongly, clasping Sophia's hand in his own. "I will hunt you down and shoot you like a dog if you give her one day's grief in her life. Do you understand?"

"Yes, sir," Justin said. "I believe every word you say, but I can tell you right now you'll never have to make good on that promise."

Milo studied the younger man's face for a full minute longer. Patsy held her breath, said a little prayer that Milo would see reason. She thought Sophia did, too. Finally Milo nodded, satisfied at last. He held out his hand. "You have my blessing," he said, "and God willing, my Juliana will add hers."

"Thank you, sir," Justin said shaking Milo's hand.

"Grandpa…" Sophia was crying, wiping her eyes,

trying to give Milo a hug and kiss at the same time. "Thank you."

Milo patted her hand, near to tears himself. "I meant every word I said but I don't want my Juliana to be upset about anything else, and God forgive me, she has been because of this. I'm ashamed of myself for causing her pain. I blame myself for her getting sick." He sniffed, pulling a big white handkerchief out of his pants pocket to wipe his nose. "Where are those doctors? I want to see her. I want to know what's going on."

The big doors glided open again. Kent and Tanya came hurrying up to where they stood in the little alcove across from the admitting desk. "We couldn't find a place to park. We ended up in one of the doctor's spaces," Tanya explained, breathless from hurrying.

"I hope he has the day off," Kent added. "Otherwise my truck's going to get towed."

"Or hope that he's a Kent Grosso fan and will give up his space for an autograph," Sophia said, her hand in Justin's, although she stayed very close to Milo.

"Hey, what about your old man?" Dean teased her. "Maybe he's a Dean Grosso fan, instead."

"Or a Justin Murphy fan," Sophia chimed in, a little giddy with relief, Patsy thought.

The Grosso men looked at each other and shook their heads. "Nah," Kent drawled. "Not yet, anyway."

Sophia opened her mouth to defend her man when Patsy caught sight of a tall, heavyset African-American man in green scrubs coming through the door that separated the treatment rooms from the admitting area. He looked at the Grosso men, one by one, his eyes widening slightly at the sight of three NASCAR Sprint Cup Series drivers in his hospital at the same time. He grinned and nodded a greeting, then his penetrating, brown gaze settled on Milo. "Mr. Milo Grosso?"

"Yes."

"I'm Doctor Maywood. I'm taking care of your wife."

Milo took a step closer leaning heavily on his cane. "How is she? How is my Juliana? Is she going to be all right?"

The doctor's smile widened. "Yes," he said. "She's going to be all right."

"But her heart. Is her heart damaged?"

"Her heart is fine," he said, putting his arm around Milo, leading him toward the swinging door through which he'd just appeared. "I'm happy to say she didn't suffer a heart attack."

"But the pain," Milo said, sounding bewildered, stopping to stare up at the taller man. "Are you sure it wasn't a heart attack?"

"Positive." He placed his arm beneath Milo's elbow and indicated the others should follow them through the swinging doors. "Her symptoms weren't caused by a heart attack."

"What else could it be? My Juliana is a strong woman. She doesn't break down easily."

"The pain was caused by stones moving into her bile duct. She had an acute gallbladder attack. She's going to be fine, but I'm afraid not until after her gallbladder is removed."

CHAPTER TWENTY

"CAN I GET YOU something to drink, Patsy?" Dean asked, coming up to her, as she stood by the window in the alcove that held a couple of vending machines, looking out over the hospital parking lot. She shook her head, declining his offer. After six hours and as many cups, she felt awash in strong hospital coffee. She didn't need any more.

The gray November day had long since faded into darkness. Tendrils of fog swirled around the streetlights; everything beyond the glass looked hazy and diffused. Still, she longed to be able to go stand outside and breathe in the cool, damp night air but Juliana was due back from the recovery room in a few minutes and she didn't want to chance missing being there when she arrived.

"Is Milo resting?" she asked, wanting to say so much more but unable to find the right words to start building a bridge over the chasm she had created between them.

"He's got his eyes closed. But I don't think he's sleeping." The surgical waiting room was equipped with a pair of big leather recliners. Since it was a holiday and no other surgeries had been scheduled, they'd had the room to themselves and it hadn't taken much persuasion to settle Milo into one of the comfortable chairs.

"I'm worried about him. This has been such a strain on him."

"He's a tough old bird," Dean said, but his voice had roughened slightly, as it always did when he was trying to keep his emotions in check.

"Who do you think was driving the truck the night Troy Murphy was killed?" She'd been thinking of the conversation between Justin and Milo during the long hours of waiting for Juliana to emerge from surgery and the question popped out almost of its own volition.

Who had been responsible for Troy Murphy's death? It had been one of the underlying questions of their marriage, another of the dark happenings in her life that sometimes had the power to keep her awake at night. Over time she had come to grudgingly accept the fact she would probably never learn the answer, just as they would never have Gina returned to them.

"I have my suspicions," Dean said.

"You do?" She turned her head unable to stop herself from looking at him. So close, all this long day, and yet he hadn't touched her once, nor she him. He was leaning against the window frame, his chin and jaw darkened by a shadow of beard, his hands shoved in the front pockets of his jeans, watching her. He was wearing another of the shirts she'd bought him for his birthday the year before, the same warm brown as his eyes. Dean hated shopping. Who would buy his clothes for him if they stayed estranged?

"You never told me that."

"What good would it have done? She'd disappeared

off the face of the earth by the time I figured it out. No one had any idea what had happened to her."

"She?" Bits and pieces of memory clicked into place in her brain and coalesced into a face and a form, a small, thin young woman with a haunted look in her eyes. "Sylvie Murphy? You think Sylvie Murphy killed her own brother-in-law?"

He nodded, looking past her right shoulder into his own thoughts. "I believe she was behind the wheel that night. Troy Murphy was every bit the bastard Milo thinks he was. He chased every woman he saw, whether they were interested or not."

Patsy shuddered with distaste. "I remember very well what he was like. The last time he tried to make a pass at me I threatened to—" She glanced around, not wanting to be overheard by any chance passersby in the hallway. "Oh, never mind, you know what I mean."

Dean grinned. "You did? I guess I wouldn't have had to threaten to do the same thing the last time I saw him then."

"It wasn't funny when it happened," Patsy said indignantly.

Dean's expression hardened. "I wasn't joking when I said it, either."

"He frightened me." Patsy's thoughts drifted back to those long ago days when Dean was just breaking into the show, still driving the dirt tracks to keep a roof over their heads while he waited for a full-time ride in the NASCAR Sprint Cup Series. She'd been pregnant with Sophia, busy raising a toddler and still, privately, mourning her lost child. Troy Murphy was a handsome man, but his looks did nothing to hide the swaggering bully inside. He ran roughshod over weaker men and made advances to every woman he met, old or young, married or single. She shivered with the memory of her distaste for him.

"I imagine we'll find out he frightened Sylvie even more than he did you." He shrugged. Sylvie Murphy had been a chance acquaintance in those days, neither of them had ever gotten to know her very well. She was a Murphy, after all. Then, as now, Grossos and Murphys stayed out of each other's way.

Until Justin and Sophia fell in love with each other and brought them into reluctant contact again.

Patsy folded her arms across her chest. "Why didn't you tell the police what you suspected? Why didn't you tell me?"

"Because you were pregnant again, remember? And I didn't want the old rumors of Connor Murphy's death to get any more play than they already were after the— accident. *NASCAR's Hatfields and McCoys. Two families. Two mysterious deaths.* God, I hate that crap." He lifted one shoulder in a negligent shrug. "Besides I didn't have any proof. Only hunches. Sylvie was gone. Disappeared into thin air. The investigation had been dropped. I figured it was better to let it go."

"What would you have done if you hadn't had an alibi, and the police had arrested you?" Even today the thought gave her chills.

"I would have told them what I just told you. I'm not so noble I would have gone to prison for something I didn't do to protect a stranger. No matter how sorry I felt for her."

Patsy shook her head. "I'm not so sure about that.

Sometimes you have this knight-in-shining-armor thing going."

"You would have set me straight fast enough."

"Yes," she said emphatically. "I would have done that. But your reputation. All these years—"

He cut her off by touching the tip of his finger to her lips. "I've lived my life the best I know how, Patsy-girl. I'm at peace with myself and with my Lord. I don't care what anyone else thinks." His voice dropped a couple of notes, roughened around the edges, and Patsy felt electricity run across her nerve endings as he dipped his head toward hers. "Except you. And you never doubted me, did you?"

She looked inward, into the deepest reaches of her heart. "Never," she whispered. "Never for a moment." He was looking at her as he always used to, tying her to him with the intensity of the love she could see shining in the deepest recesses of his eyes. *Now,* she heard her heart insisting. *Tell him how wrong you've been. How much you need him. How much you love him and want him back.* "Dean, I need to tell you—"

"Mom. Dad." It was Sophia appearing in entrance of the service alcove. "Nana's back in her room and she wants to see you."

"We're coming, Sophia."

Dean raised his hand to halt her leaving. "What, Patsy-girl? What did you want to tell me?" His voice was gentle, loverlike, but he was no longer within kissing distance, no longer close enough to keep her courage from ebbing away.

"Nothing. It was nothing. We'd better go to Nana." She turned away from him so quickly she nearly tripped and fell. He reached out, steadied her for a moment, a handful of heartbeats, no more, and then let her go. The skin beneath her shirt sleeve tingled where he'd touched her, but the pleasant sensation wasn't enough to banish the icy fear she had waited too long to try and win him back.

CHAPTER TWENTY-ONE

HE WONDERED WHAT she'd been going to say to him as they walked down the hallway toward Juliana's room. The look in her eyes had been soft, the bemused expression on her face had made him want to reach out and take her in his arms, kiss her until she was breathless and the fight had gone out of her. Then he would carry her off somewhere quiet and private and make love to her until neither of them could remember what it was they were fighting about.

He'd almost accomplished that task the night he'd won the NASCAR Sprint Cup Series championship. Would have, too, if they'd had just another hour to talk about his retirement, their plans for the future. Instead, he had made love to her again and the pleasure of it had cost him dearly. Now they were further apart than they'd ever been.

His melancholy thoughts brought them to the doorway of Juliana's hospital room. Dean hesitated for a moment before moving through the opening. He hated hospitals. Hated them with a passion. Hospitals were where you went to die. He knew it wasn't logical but he couldn't help himself. It was a gut instinct too primitive to respond to logic. He had a sneaking suspicion he wasn't the only driver who felt that way.

Patsy stepped into the room ahead of him. Kent and Tanya were already there, standing together by the window, along with Justin and Sophia. Justin stood a little removed from the others, looking almost as uncomfortable in his surroundings as Dean felt, but determined to stay by her side. Sophia was stationed in front of the array of beeping monitors that stood sentinel against the wall, scrutinizing their readouts. Milo was perched on the edge of the high bed, Juliana's right hand enfolded in his.

Dean pasted a smile on his face and walked to Juliana's side, the one with the IV stand and all the monitors, wondering whether or not he dared give her a kiss. She was propped up on pillows, a white blanket drawn up to her shoulders, her left arm strapped to a board to prevent her from disturbing the IV drips running into the back of her hand. She looked tired and worn out but no longer in pain.

"How are you feeling?" he asked, leaning down to give her a gingerly peck on the cheek.

"Not too bad," she said. "I don't hurt at all anymore. I think they're giving me something for the pain."

Sophia chuckled and waved her hand at the IV stand. "You're getting several 'somethings' for the pain, Nana," she explained. "And if you start to feel uncomfortable you only have to push the button I put in your hand and you'll get another dose of medication. You don't have to call the nurse or anything."

"I don't want to get addicted to that stuff," Juliana grumbled, peering suspiciously down at the call button-like device in her left hand.

"You won't, Nana," Sophia continued patiently. "It

has a timing device so you can't push it too often and overdose."

"I'll stay right here all night to help you with it," Milo declared.

"You'll do no such thing. I only had my gallbladder removed, not a heart transplant. I can survive the night here alone. You go home to your own bed and get some sleep."

"Always with the orders," Milo grumbled back, but he was smiling as he said it. "You should have been a general in the army."

"Oh, pooh," Juliana said dismissively. "Patsy? Where have you been? I didn't see you come in."

"I've been right here, Nana, waiting my turn." Dean stepped back, motioning her to take his place at the bedside. "We're so relieved the surgery went well."

"So am I. My gallbladder's been bad for a long time the doctor said, and I always just thought it was heartburn. I don't know why it couldn't have waited another day to blow up on me. This is not how I planned to spend Thanksgiving, I can tell you." She angled her head to return Patsy's kiss.

Patsy chuckled. "Amen to that."

Kent had been talking quietly on his cell. He flipped it shut and announced, "Nana, Heidi and Steve will be here before visiting hours are over. Larry and Crystal phoned to say they would be back in town the first thing tomorrow morning."

"They don't have to bother," Juliana said, but it was evident to Dean she was pleased his brother and nephew would be with them soon.

"They can help eat the leftovers," Kent said.

"I can't stand to have my food go to waste." Juliana closed her eyes and was quiet for so long Dean thought she might have fallen asleep. He opened his mouth to suggest they leave her to rest. They were way over the limit for visitors in the room and it was past Milo's usual bedtime.

Juliana opened her eyes before he could speak. "I was afraid I was going to die," she said to Milo.

"But you didn't, my love."

"You're going to be fine, Nana."

Juliana looked up at Sophia. "I know that now." Then her eyes settled on each of them in turn. "When the pain first hit me. Like a sledgehammer right here." She touched the middle of her chest. "I thought I was breathing my last breath and that I would go to my Maker and leave Milo behind with the terrible burden of the secret he's been keeping from me all these years."

"Hush, Juliana. You're talking nonsense," Milo said.

"I'm not," she insisted, sounding weary but determined.

"Nana, you need your rest. Whatever is on your mind you can talk to Grandpa about it tomorrow."

"The doctor said if you have a comfortable night we can take you home tomorrow afternoon," Milo hastened to add. His grandfather's eyebrows were drawn together in a frown, Dean noted. The old man was visibly agitated and seemed anxious to change the subject.

"I won't sleep a wink. How can anyone rest in a hospital with people coming and going, poking and prodding? If you do manage to doze off they come in and wake you to give you a pill or ask you how you feel or who-knows-what." Juliana paused for breath and winced as the small incisions in her abdomen felt the strain but continued fiercely. "No, Milo. You aren't going to put me off again. You have to tell me what happened all those years ago. Did you kill Connor Murphy that night? Did you run him off the road?"

"Nana? What are you saying?" The color drained from Sophia's face. She cast a quick, pleading glance over her shoulder. Dean felt a little pang around his heart when he realized she wasn't looking to him for enlightenment but to Justin.

She turned her head back to Juliana. "Why do you think Grandpa would do such a thing?"

"Because the night he died I threatened to put Connor Murphy down like a mad dog and more than one person heard me say it," Milo replied. He held Juliana's hand between his own, staring down at it, rubbing his thumb across the back of her knuckles. "And some of them were probably all too happy to tell you about it after we were married, weren't they?"

"Yes," Juliana whispered. "Did you run him off the road?"

"No," he said. "I did not."

"But you know who did."

"Yes," he said wearily. "I know."

"Tell me, Milo. Tell me, please." There were tears in Juliana's eyes. She closed them for a moment and Milo reached up to brush one away with the pad of his thumb.

"Don't cry, love."

"I can't help it. All these years I've kept it bottled up inside me. What happened that night?"

"I've kept her secret for so long," he said, following his own train of thought. "So long."

Dean could barely hear the old man's words over the hammering of his own heart. More secrets to be revealed. He had never realized his family harbored so many until these last few months. First Troy Murphy and now Justin's great-uncle Connor. After so long remaining a mystery would they learn the true stories of how both men had died on the very same day?

"It was Frances, wasn't it?" Juliana no longer seemed to be aware of the others in the room. Her universe had narrowed to the small space surrounding her and the man she loved.

Milo nodded, tears leaking from the corner of his eyes. He fumbled for his handkerchief, brought it out and blew his nose. "My poor, gentle Frances. I promised her for Alfonso's sake, for the grandbabies she loved so dearly, that I would take her secret to my grave."

His grandmother. A woman Dean knew only from faded photographs and black-and-white home movies, had been responsible for a man's death? His grandmother had killed Connor Murphy? Dean couldn't wrap his mind around it. He stood staring blindly at the back of Milo's head, his thoughts slamming around in his brain as though he'd cut a tire on Turn Four at Talladega at close to 180 miles an hour and spun into the wall. The words hit him with the same force, the same shock to the system.

"Why, Milo? She must have had a reason."

"Grandpa, please. Explain this to us," Sophia pleaded. Justin brushed past Dean, rooted as he was to the floor, and rested his hands on Sophia's shoulders. She leaned against him, connecting with her life partner, with the man she loved.

An overwhelming urge to feel Patsy nestled in his arms, lending him her strength, her love, surged through him, a wave of need and longing that dwarfed what he'd been feeling before.

"Frances was the kindest, gentlest woman who ever lived," Milo said, looking around at all of them. "You never got to know her, any of you, but that is the truth."

"So different from me," Juliana said.

"So very different," Milo agreed. "And I loved her. But in a different way than I love you."

"I know, Milo. I've never been jealous of her. How could I be? She gave us Alfonso, and our wonderful boys."

Milo patted her hand. "You were alike in one way. She had a fierce pride and loyalty to the people she loved. She was angry, angrier than I'd ever seen her when it was found out Connor doctored his fuel. It hurt my chances to win the championship and I... God forgive me, I didn't take it well. It upset her. It upset her terribly. They didn't have near the kind of testing they do nowadays. Lots of stuff like that went on and was never found out."

"Was that the year Connor won Daytona?" Justin asked quietly.

Milo turned his head, gave him a long look and nodded. "It was. Beat me out by a quarter of a second. I had a damned good car that year but it couldn't stack up against one runnin' on rocket fuel.

"By then I was in my forties. Spent some of my best

racing years in Europe fighting the Germans, but I'm not complaining. Frances and I had bought the farm after the war. We started raising quarter horses and we did okay. There wasn't big money in NASCAR in those days but we managed. I'd had a couple of bad wrecks. It was time to move on. Besides," he said, his voice cracking with emotion, "I had a son who was going to follow in my footsteps."

"The old guys, the ones who remember, tell me he was a hell of a driver," Kent said, clearing his throat when the words cracked around the edges. Tanya reached out and wrapped both hands around his arm, leaning her cheek on his shoulder.

"He would have been one of the best," Sophia said loyally. "Dad's always told me that, Grandpa."

Milo nodded. "Alfonso was a fine driver, my pride and joy. I figured someday he would win the championship for me. The closest I came was second. I didn't know he would be taken from us so soon, and his beautiful Gina with him. But that was all in the future.

"I did my best to move on after that season, but Frances kept all the hurt and the anger inside her. One night we were out at the dirt track where I still liked to watch the young guns earn their Sunday money. I was helping a couple of them work on their cars." He looked down at his hands, joined with Juliana's, but it was apparent he was seeing what had taken place so long ago. "Connor was there, too, bragging about his big win at Daytona. It took all the willpower I had to keep from picking up a tire iron and taking it to him. But I didn't. I wasn't going to jail for him.

"Frances had been feeling poorly and she said she

felt another one of the blinding headaches she'd been having coming on. She wanted to go home, but God help me I thought I had to stay at the track and defend my honor if Connor kept it up. But just about the same time Frances drove off in my truck, Connor took off on that big old motorcycle of his. I didn't think much of it but later Frances told me he cut her off at a crossroads a ways out of town, slammed to a stop, then jumped out to ask her what it was like to be married to a damned yellow coward who wouldn't even defend his good name? He bragged about doctoring his fuel.

"Then he took off like a bat out of hell. Frances followed him. She told me later the pain in her head was so bad it made her a little crazy. She wasn't thinking straight. She was a little thing. Barely a hundred pounds dripping wet. She was no match for Connor, but she wanted to catch him to make him apologize for what he'd said. What he'd done.

"That was my favorite truck she was driving. I'd done a lot of customizing. It could outrun just about anything out there and it didn't take Frances long to catch up with Connor. They were out near the lake, on a high bluff looking down over the water. Frances came up behind the motorcycle. She stayed on his back wheel. They kept going that way for a couple of miles, only meeting one or two cars, enough, though, that someone recognized my truck."

"Did she run him off the road?" Juliana whispered. "Did she deliberately send him over the edge of that ravine?"

"She didn't know what she was doing," Milo said softly, and then spoke with more volume and strength. "I believe that. I believe that with all my heart. It was the sickness, the cancer had gotten into her brain, made her half-crazy with pain. It can do that to a person, can't it, Sophia? Make them do things they'd never do otherwise?"

"Yes, Grandpa. It can happen," Sophia said.

"When she hit his back wheel with the truck Connor skidded out and went over the edge. Frances told me she could hear him scream for a long way down. She couldn't believe what she had done. She was in shock. She kept on going, drove damned near all the way around the lake before she got up her courage to go back and try and find the bike. When she got there the police and ambulance were on the scene. She was still in a lot of pain. She was afraid if she had to talk to them she'd say something wrong, give herself away, so she turned off on a little side road and worked her way back to town.

"I was waiting up for her. She never stayed out late like that. Never. She was still crying and shaking when she got back to the farm. I could see something terrible had happened. I just held out my arms and she fell into them. I held her for a long, long time coaxing the whole story out of her. She begged me not to tell anyone. She was so frightened of going to jail, of causing a scandal that would reflect on Alfonso and Gina, on all of us."

"Sophia's right. It was the cancer getting into her brain that made her do it, I think," Juliana said, tears streaming down her face. "She couldn't have been herself."

"She was never right after that night. The headaches got so bad she couldn't see. We took her to the specialist. They said there was nothing they could do. The cancer was everywhere by then. They gave her so many drugs for the pain, but they didn't help. Her last weeks of life were hell on earth. She was consumed with guilt and the pain. She died believing she would go to hell for what she had done and there was no way I could convince her otherwise, give her even that much peace of mind."

Sophia turned her head into Justin's chest and wept. Dean knew from his daughter's reaction that his suspicions regarding Sylvie Murphy and Troy Murphy were correct. And he also understood why Justin and Hugo, all the Murphys, were banding together to keep her secret from becoming public knowledge, even though it was one of their own blood that she had accidentally killed. He suspected it was the same fierce protective instinct that had driven Milo to keep his troubling secret for close to fifty years.

"All this time I've let the gossips and the rumormongers have their field day. I didn't care. I mourned her deeply. I stayed away from racing, except to watch my son. And then one summer I went to Nashville to buy horses for my farm and the man I was dealing for them with took me to a nightclub and I saw a young, beautiful woman walk up on the stage and start to sing and I fell in love all over again. I never thought she would love me back, a broken down ex-G-man, a failed NASCAR driver, a grandfather, for God's sake. But she did. And I'm still in love with her, all these years later."

"And I'm still in love with you. Oh, Milo. Why didn't you tell me all this a long time ago. Why didn't you let me help you bear the burden of it?"

"Because I was foolish and I thought I was protecting you. I didn't want to fail you the way I failed her."

"You didn't fail me. You've never failed me. But now we can finally put this behind us. Lay it to rest. Let her rest in peace."

"Yes," he said. "All of them. All of our lost ones can rest in peace."

Dean heard Patsy's breath catch on a sigh. She was thinking of their lost daughter again. Patsy wasn't at peace, wouldn't be until she had purged her grief and loss and mother's guilt, the way Juliana had begged Milo to do. He knew that because he needed the same redemption. He moved to enfold her in his arms without thinking, without considering the consequences of the act. She stiffened momentarily and he braced himself for her to pull away, to take the final, irrevocable step of rejecting him and their marriage.

He held his breath, waiting. Then she relaxed against him for just a moment, a handful of heartbeats before she straightened her spine and moved out of his embrace. But it was enough. It was a beginning, a first step to healing the breach between them and he intended to take full advantage of the opportunity.

CHAPTER TWENTY-TWO

"IS MILO SLEEPING?" Patsy asked, turning from the sink as she heard Dean enter the kitchen. So much had happened in the twelve hours since they'd abandoned their preparations for Thanksgiving dinner that it had been a little disorienting when they returned to the farm to see the table set with Juliana's heavy silver flatware, a traditional cornucopia of mums and gourds and dried wheat and grasses still looking fresh and lovely in its place at the center of the long, pine table, the counters covered with plates of bread and rolls, the refrigerators crammed full of side dishes and the turkey waiting to be reheated and enjoyed.

"He's snoring away like a band saw," Dean reported, settling onto a stool. He lifted the plastic film from a dish of nut bread, broke off a corner of the sweet, moist bread and offered it to her.

She shook her head. "Thanks, no. You eat it. He's exhausted, poor soul. I'm so glad Dr. Maywood was able to talk him into coming home with us."

Shortly after Milo's startling revelation of the details of the night a half century before when Connor Murphy died, Heidi and Steve had arrived in Juliana's room bearing a colorful bouquet of helium balloons and a huge stuffed teddy bear. Juliana pooh-poohed the stuffed animal as a silly gift for an old woman, but insisted it be propped up on the foot of her bed to keep her company through the night.

Heidi and Steve had stayed just long enough to be reassured that Juliana was coming along okay, give her their love and Larry and Crystal's, along with a couple of hugs, and then they left because the nurses were beginning to look askance at the number of people in the room. A few minutes later Dr. Maywood appeared on his evening rounds, still wearing a surgical cap and scrubs beneath a long white coat, shooed the rest of them out into the hallway while he checked Juliana's incisions, and then let them back in.

"She's doing great," he'd said. "Her vital signs are excellent. She's not in pain. If she has a restful night I don't see any reason why she can't go home tomorrow afternoon as we'd planned. Give yourself six weeks to recuperate—"

"Six weeks?" Juliana protested.

"Okay. Three, but I mean it. Take it easy until Christmas. A cholecystectomy is nothing like it used to be but it's still a serious surgery. Do you understand, Mrs. Grosso?"

"All right," she acquiesced with obvious reluctance.

"Excellent," he said heartily. He placed a hand on each knee and boosted himself out of the bedside chair. "I'll drop in on you after lunch and if you're feeling well enough I'll sign the discharge papers then."

"I'll be feeling well enough, don't you think I won't," Juliana said, getting the last word.

And then the doctor had cemented his place in her

affections by asking Milo for his autograph. Not Dean, the new NASCAR Sprint Cup Series champion, nor Kent nor Justin. Only Milo. "I'm a real classic NASCAR fan," he said, rifling his pocket before handing Milo a prescription pad to sign. "My dad is, too. His birthday's coming up. I'll have this framed and give it to him then. It will make his day, I can tell you."

"I'll bet he'll be surprised to find I'm still above ground," Milo huffed, but it was easy to see he was flattered by the recognition.

"He used to tell me about watching you and the other great ones drive on dirt tracks back in the day." He beamed down at Milo's autograph and carefully placed it in his pocket. "Is it true you were an FBI agent back then? That you knew J. Edgar Hoover?"

"That's correct," Milo said, sitting a little straighter. "But that was a long, long time ago. Before the war."

"You were in the war, too?"

"European theater," Milo said. "D-day plus two all the way to Berlin in forty-five."

"My dad was a Marine. Is a Marine," Dr. Maywood corrected himself with a grin. "No such thing as an ex-Marine. Vietnam. Two tours."

"Tough going there, too."

"And when you came back from the war you went back to racing."

Milo glanced at Juliana. "For a while, but my best days were behind me."

"But you were there at the beginning of NASCAR. You've seen it all. Daytona when they raced on the beach. All the great old tracks."

"Won at a few of them, too," Milo interjected.

"More than one or two if I remember correctly. You've done it all. You should write a book, sir," the doctor had declared. "It would be a bestseller for sure."

"I've told him that for years," Juliana seconded, her eyes shining with pride and love. "He's got a lot of stories to tell."

"But no more secrets," Milo had said.

"No more secrets," Juliana had echoed, "only things best kept to ourselves."

But she and Dean still had secrets and Patsy wanted desperately to be free of the burden of them.

"What are you thinking about?" he asked quietly.

She blinked bringing her attention back to the here and now, then gave in to the temptation to lose herself in the newfound warmth of his eyes. She had lost her courage earlier when he'd asked her what she was thinking, what she wanted, but this time she would not. It was too important to her. He was too important to her. She had never expected to be alone with him again this way, in their own home, in the quiet dark hours of the night with nothing to distract them. It was like another small miracle to add to the blessing of the larger one they'd experienced that day.

"I was thinking about everything that's happened since we walked out of this room earlier," she said simply.

"A hell of a day," he agreed.

"Are you okay?" she asked. He looked bone-weary, the way he did after a long hard race, as though he was operating on a reservoir of strength he called on when it was necessary. Without thinking he reached up and rubbed the back of his neck, frowning a little. She clutched the dish towel harder to keep from offering to massage the pain away.

"I'm as tired as Milo," he confessed. "It's pretty hard to absorb all of it."

"Are you okay with what Milo told us about your grandmother?" He didn't often speak of Milo's first wife. Or much about his parents, either. They had died when he was so young his memories of them were few. Milo and Juliana had been the only parents he knew.

"Yeah," he said. "I guess." He reached for another bite of nut bread, as though he, too, might need something to do with his hands. "I've only ever known her from her pictures. That's to say I didn't know her at all. Milo didn't talk about her much, or Mom and Dad, either. Most of my memories of them come from Nana."

"She loved your mother. She was so pleased when we chose her name for our baby girl." Her throat closed for a moment but she fought the urge to cry. Now was not the time for mourning what was lost but for renewing what she had come so close to losing. "I'm sorry Frances's last weeks on earth were so unhappy."

"I am, too. But there's nothing we can do about that now."

"Except protect her memory just as Milo has done all these years. The Murphys will have to be told what happened to Connor, but I doubt they would want it made public knowledge any more than we do."

"Especially with Sylvie's reputation to protect. That's fine with me. All of us, put the past behind us. Bury it deep. No more Hatfields and McCoys of stock car racing."

"Amen." Her heart rate picked up speed and she felt her chest tighten again. "I want to tell Sophia and Kent about Gina as soon as possible, too."

He stood up and came around the island, stopping just short of taking her in his arms. "We can ask them to come out for breakfast before we go back to the hospital. Justin and Tanya should be here, too. We'll tell them everything that happened."

"So they won't forget her," Patsy said, letting the tears she'd been holding back all day fall, so that they might wash away a little of the pain.

"We will never forget her. And they won't, either." He reached out and took the towel she'd been twisting between her fingers. "Ever."

"Don't leave me tonight, Dean," she whispered. "I don't want to be alone."

"I don't plan to," he said simply and lowered his head for a kiss.

Hope bloomed inside her heart, made her a little giddy, a little dizzy. She clung to him. "It truly has been a day of Thanksgiving, you know," she said mistily. "I was so afraid that we were going to lose Nana. I'm not ready for that. I'm so thankful she's going to be all right."

"We all are. And I'm thankful we are here. Now. Together again," he said, enfolding her in his arms.

She clung to him, rejoiced in the hardness of bone and muscle, the warmth of his skin beneath her cheek. She could feel her heart rate accelerate, begin to hammer against her breastbone, echo in her ears. "Are we together, Dean?" she asked him. "Can we just pick up the threads of our marriage as it they were strands of yarn that can be knitted back together and go on as if nothing had happened?"

"No," he said, leaning closer. "Because it all did happen. This whole damned, long, lonely summer happened. We can't ignore that but we can get past it. Is that what you want to do, Patsy-girl, put it behind us and go on together?"

"If you'll have me back. I've been such a fool these last couple of weeks."

"I've been a fool a lot longer than that."

"I'm so sorry for the way I behaved the morning after you won the championship. I don't know what happened to me. I don't usually jump to wrongheaded conclusions that way."

"It might have been that your mind was somewhere else?" he said. "That was some pretty incredible lovemaking."

"Dean!" She felt the color rush to her face and dropped her head onto his chest to hide her embarrassment. "What a way to talk."

He lifted her chin with the tips of his fingers. "Sorry," he said, grinning, and she guessed he wasn't sorry at all, and neither was she. It had been the most incredible night they had in years. Maybe it had affected her thinking for a little while? But she'd never admit to it. "That was a little out of line. I apologize. But it was fantastic. It's just that after what we shared that night I thought that we'd never misunderstand each other again."

"I thought we never would, either."

He rubbed the tip of his nose against hers. "We both should have known better. That's not the way we work, is it? We argue. We make up. We come to an agreement and we make love."

"That's our formula," she agreed smiling. "Worked pretty well for thirty years."

"Worth giving it another try, I think." He lowered his head and kissed her lightly on the lips. "I've missed you so damned much," he said. "These last months have been hell. I don't want to be separated again a day in our lives."

A fresh batch of tears stung her eyes and blurred her vision. "Never. Not another day."

"I'll announce my retirement officially during Champions Week. I've already talked to the Smooth-tone Music people. They'll stay with Cargill-Grosso Racing if we can come up with a driver to take my place."

"You're the best there is. Replacing you won't be easy."

"Damned right it won't be easy." He grinned and she smiled back, reaching up on tiptoe to bring their mouths together again.

"It's going to be hard giving up your ride."

"Hell, I know that, but I've done what I set out to do even if it did take me twenty years longer than I planned. Time to move on. Time to find a new challenge."

"Do you really want to go ahead with buying the rest of the team from Alan? Even after the way I blew up at you for telling the radio announcers you weren't going to retire? What kind of a team owner will I make? Flying into a rage and ordering you out of the house—"

"I walked out of the house," he corrected her. "Damned fool that I am."

She ignored him. "—instead of seeing it for the savvy business maneuver it was?"

"I guess I'll just have to take my chances," he said, lifting her off the floor and spinning her in a circle. "Because I don't intend to take on that challenge without my best friend, my only love, by my side." This time the kiss was slow and thorough and it left her breathless when it was over. "There's one more thing I want to tell you."

"What?" she said clinging to him, dizzy with happiness and hope for the future.

"I love what you've done to your hair."

EPILOGUE

"Wow. IF YOUR MOM can put on a soiree like this with only five days' notice no wonder you want her to plan our wedding," Justin said, looking around him at the transformed main floor of Cargill Motors. Gone were the oversized toolboxes, the car chassis in various stages of assembly, the shop tools and air guns and team members in cotton uniforms and work boots. Everyone in the room was dressed in their Sunday best, as though rehearsing for the NASCAR awards banquet taking place in ten days' time. "I never would have thought you could have any kind of party beyond beer and bratwurst in a garage, but this is pretty swank."

"It does look nice, doesn't it," Sophia said with pardonable pride, taking a glass of champagne from a passing, tuxedo-clad waiter. "It's amazing what you can do with what you have on hand."

Patsy had sweet-talked the guys in the shop into building a framework to hold sheets of plastic that looked like old-fashioned tin ceiling tiles. She'd had them spray-painted silver and topped by a canopy of shimmering fabric suspended from the high ceiling beams, then arranged the ten-foot-tall sections to partition off a portion of the huge garage area into a smaller, more intimate space. Framed black-and-white prints of Alan and Dean in cars they'd driven years before hung in front of the silver backdrop. Dean's Smoothtone Music car sat shining and pristine at the entrance to the party area, the NASCAR Sprint Cup Series championship trophy set on the roof, backed up by hundreds of helium balloons in blue, white and gold, his racing colors.

Rotating spotlights trained on the trophy sent sparks of light shooting out over the two hundred assembled guests browsing the buffet, conversing at the small, round tables scattered over the floor, drinking champagne and beer and vintage wines with impressive pedigrees. Those who weren't talking or dancing to the deejay's music were eating canapés and various imported cheeses. There was even a sushi bar for the daring. Thankfully, as far as Justin was concerned, more substantial fare could be found on the other side of the silver screens, barbecue and baked beans, corn on the cob, brownies and pecan pie.

"What do you think? Want to get married here?" Justin asked, only half-joking, frowning down at the seaweed-wrapped concoction Sophia had snuck onto his plate when he wasn't looking.

"No," she said emphatically. "And I don't want to get married at Fulcrum's garage, either, so don't suggest that next."

"We could make it a double wedding on the beach with Kent and Tanya?"

She looked thoughtful for a moment, then shook her head. "I want to get married out by the lake," she declared, licking her fingers.

"Yuck."

"What do you mean 'yuck'? It's beautiful at your place."

"I meant this thing." Justin dropped the sushi on her plate, spearing a hunk of her barbecue with his fork. "Let's trade."

She rolled her eyes. "Sushi is good. You should broaden your horizons."

"They're broad enough, thanks." He wolfed down the barbecue, smacked his lips and made another stab with his fork, but Sophia was too quick for him.

"Go get your own," she said, holding him back with a hand on his chest.

"Did you mean that about getting married at the lake?" he asked before he could think better of it. "It's beautiful out there at Easter time." Easter weekend was one of the few open dates in the race season. And if he had to have a full ceremony wedding, as opposed to the drive-thru wedding chapel the weekend they were racing in Vegas, then the lake wasn't a bad alternative.

"Yes, I meant it," she said, pouncing. "And I think an Easter wedding would be lovely. I'll talk to Mom about it the first chance I get."

Justin swallowed hard, wondering for a moment if the barbecue was stuck in his throat. They'd really gone and done it. Set a date. "You're sure?" he asked, laying his hand across hers, looking down at the diamond-and-sapphire engagement ring she finally felt free to wear, the stone the same color as the sexy little off-the-shoulder dress she was wearing.

"I am positive," she said. "Let's go tell Grandpa and Nana before they leave." Even though it had been little more than a week since her surgery, Juliana had insisted on attending, at least for a short while, the combination retirement and change-of-ownership party that Patsy had put together in record time. She wasn't, however, making the trip to New York City for Champions Week, which was only a few days away. She wasn't happy about it but she had bowed to Milo's wishes so she would be fully recovered in time for Kent and Tanya's wedding and the Christmas holidays.

The elderly couple were enthroned in a pair of leather wing chairs, holding court as far from the video-deejay Patsy had hired for the evening's entertainment as they could manage. The chairs, Justin noticed, wouldn't have looked out of place in a Fortune 500 boardroom. "Maybe I should rethink your dad's offer to come over to Cargill-Grosso when he and your mom take over," Justin whispered into Sophia's ear as they waited for Juliana and Milo to finish up their conversation with a middle-aged woman, who, Sophia informed him, was Alan Cargill's long-time secretary. "We don't have anything like those chairs at Fulcrum."

"They are baronial, I agree," Sophia said under her breath. Alan's secretary left Milo and Juliana with a wave of her hand and headed for the bar.

"Here, give me that." Sophia plucked his plate from his hand and set them on an empty table. Moving swiftly, she towed him across the room. "Grandpa. Nana. Guess what? Justin and I have decided to be married Easter Sunday. We want to have an outdoor wedding at his place at the lake. What do you think?"

"Wonderful," Juliana laughed, leaning up to accept

Sophia's kiss on her cheek. "Congratulations! Both of you."

"Thank you, ma'am," Justin said, taking the beringed hand she held out to him.

"You're not going to get away without giving me a kiss, too," she said, pointing to her cheek. A dozen gold bracelets chimed on her wrist as she moved her arm. "You are a very lucky man, Justin Murphy, don't ever forget it," she whispered as he bent to do her bidding.

"I don't intend to, ma'am. Not for a minute."

"Grandpa?" Sophia said, not quite as confidently.

"Can't talk you out of marrying this Murphy spawn, eh?" he grumbled.

"No, sir. I've made up my mind. It's him or nobody."

Milo scowled up at Justin. "You two going to give us some great-great-grandbabies to liven up our dull existence?"

"Three or four at least," she assured him. Justin swallowed hard again. Three or four? He'd figured two. Well, hell, why not, he thought, taking a swig from his champagne flute. If the girls looked like Sophia and the boys wanted to race, he'd welcome half a dozen of them.

Sophia knelt beside the big chair and took Milo's hand between her own. "We'll name our first little girl Gina," she said, her eyes shimmering with tears. "For Dad's mother. And for my big sister."

"It's good we can speak of her now," Milo said, his voice raspy with emotion. "It's good your mother and father told you and Kent about her. About the terrible thing that happened in that hospital."

"I wish they had told us sooner. Years ago," Sophia said, tears glistening in her blue eyes. There was still a faint note of disbelief in her voice, Justin noted, as though she were not quite ready to accept the finality of Dean and Patsy's baby, her sister, being lost to them all forever.

Justin, as well as Kent's fiancée, Tanya, had been present at the farm the day after Thanksgiving. He had been glad to see that Sophia's parents had reconciled sometime in the preceding twenty-four hours, but he hadn't expected what came next. As they waited for Steve and Crystal to chauffeur Milo and Juliana home from the hospital, Dean and Patsy had told their children about their lost sister. It had been an emotional scene, and the pain of unleashed loss he'd glimpsed in the future in-laws' eyes as they recounted their sad tale would stay with him forever.

"I have a sister?" Sophia had whispered, her blue eyes unbelieving, tears streaming down her cheeks as she knelt by Patsy's chair, taking her mother's hand between her own.

"Yes," Patsy had said, crying, too. "A big sister. Gina. Kent's twin. I'm so sorry we didn't tell you before. I didn't even know there were going to be two babies. It was such a miracle. And so frightening. We were so young. And I was so scared. And then. She was just gone." She'd lifted her hand in a helpless gesture. "Disappeared in the blink of an eye. In a heartbeat. And we couldn't find her no matter how hard we searched, how long we searched. And dear Lord, we did try so hard. It hurts so much to talk of her, still. About the kidnapping—" Her voice had

broken then, and only when Dean had placed both his big hands on her shoulders and she'd laid her cheek against his knuckles for a moment had she found the courage to continue. "But she's gone, Sophia. Not just kidnapped, but dead. They told us so when they broke up the baby-stealing ring months later. There's a grave in Mexico—I've never had the courage to go...."

She had looked up at Kent then, her eyes pleading. Sophia's brother had looked as shell-shocked as Justin felt. Had to have been even more torn up inside. How could he not, finding out he had a twin sister after so many years?

"Forgive us," Patsy had said, holding out her hand.

"There's nothing to forgive," Kent had said. "I just wish you and Dad had told us sooner."

"She's been in my heart every moment." Dean had made a sound deep in his throat and Patsy had covered his hand with hers.

"She's been in our hearts, our thoughts, every day." Patsy's voice had broken completely and the tears had streamed silently down her cheeks as Sophia wrapped her arms around her mother's waist and sobbed.

"Some hurts are so deep and painful they can't be easily put into words," Milo said, pulling Justin from his thoughts, giving voice to Justin's own conclusion as to why Dean and Patsy had kept their terrible loss secret for so long.

"But if you love each other you try," Juliana answered, leaning forward to cover their hands with her own. She held out her other hand to Justin, including him in the family circle. "Share the love. Share the happiness. But also share the pain to cut it in half. And don't keep secrets from each other."

"We hear you, Nana. We're partners, Justin and I." Sophia looked up at him, her love for him plain to see. He felt like the luckiest man in the world.

"Juliana and I wish you nothing but happiness and long life."

"That's what I want, too, Grandpa." She blinked away the tears, smiled wide and confidently. "And one of those—" she gestured at the NASCAR Sprint Cup Series championship trophy shining beneath the spotlights "—to put on our mantel."

Her words faltered into silence. She turned to Justin, her expression now slightly apprehensive. "They're here," she said. "Hugo and Sylvie. They're here."

He turned to follow her line of sight. Sure enough, his uncle and his new wife were standing, hand in hand, a short distance from the buffet table, Hugo protectively close to Sylvie, his expression polite but guarded. Behind them Justin caught a glimpse of his sister and Peyton Reese. Rachel looked just as apprehensive as Sophia.

"Justin, what does this mean?" Sophia whispered. "I…I don't understand?"

He shrugged. "I'll be damned if I know." He figured this face-off would come sooner or later. He just hadn't expected it in such a public place. All of Dean and Kent's team members were here tonight, as well as a number of other drivers and their wives and girlfriends, a couple of NASCAR officials, more than a couple of media types—a lot more. Whatever happened, the result would be all over Charlotte by midnight.

Milo and Juliana had both risen from their chairs. The old man held out his arm for his wife and together they began walking toward the new arrivals. Justin braced himself, worried that Milo would make a scene. As if they'd been summoned telepathically, Dean and Patsy appeared behind Sophia. Kent and Tanya came into view on his left. From the corner of his eye he saw Larry Grosso and his son move closer to make the family circle complete.

Milo Grosso walked up to Hugo and offered his hand. "Welcome," he said, his voice strong and filled with the dignity of his years. "For a great-granddaughter and her young man's sake we're glad you could be with us tonight."

Sophia caught Justin's hand and squeezed so hard he almost yelped. "Oh, Granddad, you sweetie," she whispered. "Thank you. Thank you." She squeezed his hand again, even harder than before.

Enlightenment dawned. This wasn't shaping up to be the gunfight at the OK Corral, NASCAR style. It was the burying of the hatchet between the Grossos and the Murphys. A public blessing for his and Sophia's future together.

"Thank you," Hugo said, carefully taking Milo's frail hand in his much larger one. "We're glad to be here." Justin felt a little light-headed. A little drunk with relief and happiness. It was over. Before his eyes decades of hard feelings were coming to an end. Around them heads swiveled, turned in their direction. Murmurs of astonishment rose above the music as people began to realize they were witnessing NASCAR history.

"Good," Milo said, inclining his head in a courtly, old-fashioned bow. "You know my Juliana, I think."

"Ma'am," Hugo said, gravely polite, holding out his hand. "Thank you for inviting us."

"Juliana," she said, beaming at Milo, her eyes sparkling with tears. "Call me Juliana. And you must be Sylvie," she said, turning her smile on Hugo's wife.

"Yes, Mrs. Grosso," she replied. "I'm Sylvie Murphy. It's…it's nice to meet you." Sylvie managed a smile of her own and held out her hand. It was trembling slightly. Justin realized what an ordeal this must be for Hugo's wife, but she was handling it with aplomb.

"Mrs. Grosso? Pooh. No one calls me Mrs. Grosso." Juliana clasped Sylvie's slender hand between both her own, her eyes sparkling as brightly as the diamonds on her fingers and wrists now that Milo had fulfilled the promise he'd made her in the hospital to put the past behind them. "You must both call me Juliana. After all, we're family now."

THE FAINT SOUNDS of music and laughter from the party on the garage floor seeped through the walls of Alan's office as he scrawled his signature on each of three separate documents marked by small colored arrows above where Patsy and Dean had already signed. "It's done," he said, straightening from his task. "You two are now the owners of this race team. Congratulations." He held out his hand to Dean and shook it strongly. "If you're not going to be driving my race cars any longer I'll be glad to see you behind my desk."

"I'll do my best to keep winning races for the team, Alan, no matter where I'm sitting."

"Hell, I know that," the big man said, grinning. "And with Patsy in charge of the money end of things you might even turn a profit—someday." Placing his big scarred hands gently on Patsy's shoulders he leaned down to kiss her cheek. "Congratulations, Mrs. Grosso."

"Thank you, Alan. We'll do our best to make you proud, too."

"I already am."

Dean eyed the bottle of champagne chilling in one of his trophies taken out of the glass cases that lined one wall of the garage floor to do double duty as a wine cooler. "Shall we drink to the future before we go back to our guests?" he asked, picking up the towel-wrapped green bottle.

"I'd rather have a shot of bourbon," Alan responded, going to the big credenza behind the desk and touching a portion of the ornate carving. A panel slid sideways and a small, but fully equipped, bar appeared.

"I'll be damned," Dean said, whistling through his teeth. "Never knew that was there."

"Don't use it often," Alan said, "but it comes in handy on special occasions like this. One of the perks of being the boss." He took two glasses from the shelf and a decanter of bourbon the same color of amber as the cowl-necked sweater Patsy was wearing over a slim black skirt.

Alan poured two generous shots of bourbon while Dean dealt with the champagne, filling a flute for Patsy. Alan raised his glass in a toast. "Here's to a long and successful future for this team. And here's to my driver, winner of the NASCAR Sprint Cup Series championship.

May that wonderful trophy down there be the first of many for the two of you as owners of Cargill-Grosso Racing."

"Amen to that," Dean said.

They touched their glasses in a toast and drained them in silence. "Now," Alan said, "I'm officially retired but we still have guests to entertain. And since you didn't manage to talk your future son-in-law into coming on board I'm going downstairs and take another shot at getting Kent to come drive for us."

"Don't offer him the moon," Patsy said.

"Hey, you hired me to recruit drivers for the new team. It takes money to make money."

"Is it too late to rethink this particular strategy?" Dean asked.

"Yep."

"I was afraid of that."

"I'll give you two a few minutes alone to contemplate the enormity of what you've just done," He grinned, saluted them both with his refilled glass and sauntered out of the office without looking back.

"He made that look easy," Dean said after a few moments of silence. He hoped he could step out of the driver's seat with half as much class when the time came to go public with his retirement. He looked around the office he had sat in so many times, but always on the other side of the desk, always as the driver, not the boss, not the man who made the decisions and took all the heat.

"A very class act, our friend."

A quick knock on the door was followed by it opening once more. "This place is Grand Central Station," Dean mumbled under his breath.

Kent stepped inside the office. "You're supposed to be downstairs making a speech," he reminded them. "The Murphys look like they've had enough bonding and camaraderie for the evening, but I figure they don't want to give the impression they're poor sports walking out before the big announcement."

"I can't believe they came." Patsy turned her head and caught Dean's gaze for a moment. "When did you invite them? Did you invite them?" She turned her hand palm up. "How did you talk them into coming?"

"It was Granddad's idea," Dean explained. "He promised Juliana he'd bury the hatchet after Justin told us the truth about how his father died. Milo puts a lot of store in keeping his word. We figured the best way to accomplish that was to get right to it, so we took a six-pack of beer and a fifth of whiskey to the Fulcrum garage one night last week and sat down with Hugo and cleared the air," he finished.

"You're kidding me." Patsy's eyes widened with surprise. "You didn't breathe a word of this to me."

"We weren't sure how Hugo would react. Besides, it was a guy thing. You wouldn't understand." She gave him a sharp look and he backed off, finishing his story quickly. "Luckily, Hugo was as tired of this whole feud as we are. And he wants Justin and Sophia to be happy. I think that's what really sealed the deal. Hugo raised Justin. He wants what's best for him. And besides, we're going to be sharing grand-kids or great-nieces and -nephews one day, you know."

"Just like that the Grosso-Murphy feud is settled," Kent said, one eyebrow raised.

"Just like that," Dean repeated. "Do you have a problem with that?"

"Nope," his son replied, a smile spreading across his face. "Not a single one."

"Good. Just wanted to make sure we're all agreed on this."

"The bad blood between us officially ends tonight," Patsy stated, giving him a glorious smile that made him thank his lucky stars all over again that she had come back to him. "Thank you for taking the first step, Dean."

"From now on the past is dead," Kent said, then picked up Patsy's champagne flute and lifted it in a toast.

"And how and why Connor and Troy died is going to stay just as deeply buried." Patsy said, her eyes locked on his.

"Dead and buried," Kent promised. He indicated the contracts Patsy was still holding. "The deed is done, I take it?"

"Signed, sealed and delivered."

"You own a NASCAR Sprint Series Cup team." He came forward and gave Patsy a hug. "Congratulations, Mom." He reached out and shook Dean's hand. "Congratulations, Dad."

"Thanks, son."

"I passed Alan in the hall. He wants to talk to me. Want to tell me what that's all about?" His grin grew wider.

"You'll find out soon enough," Patsy said. "Will you go and help entertain the Murphys with Justin and Sophia for a few minutes? Your father and I have a couple of loose ends to tie up here before we come back down to the party."

"Sure, Mom. Anything to get on the bosses' good side." He touched his fingers to his forehead in a quick salute as he shut the door behind him.

"He's going to drive a hard bargain," Dean said, shaking his head.

"Alan can handle him. And he's worth every penny." Patsy tapped the contracts she was holding into alignment. "What are you thinking?" she asked as she walked to the wall safe.

"I'm wondering if we haven't lost our minds," he said honestly, coming to stand behind her as she spun the dials and locked the proof of their ownership safely away.

She stared at the safe a moment. "We own a NASCAR Sprint Cup Series team," she said, a note of wonder in her voice as she turned to face him. "Us. Patsy and Dean Grosso."

"We are also in hock up to our eyeballs," he said dryly.

"Just like the old days," she said, but of course it wasn't. This was a multimillion-dollar business deal not a secondhand motor home, or even buying a NASCAR Nationwide Series car. He felt the palms of his hands go damp but then he looked into her shining blue eyes and the momentary doubt faded away. "Money doesn't buy happiness," she said sagely. "Sometimes you're better off without it."

"Well, I'm feeling downright delirious and giddy right now, 'cause there ain't no better way on earth to watch money disappear than to pour it into a race car."

"It's not going to disappear," she said, wrapping her arms around his neck, drawing his head down for a kiss. "I'll see to that."

She would, too. He didn't have a moment's doubt about it. "I love you, Patsy-girl. I always have. I always will." He'd learned one thing over the months of their separation. He could never tell her enough times that he loved her.

"I love you, Dean. I always have. I always will."

"We make a hell of a team. Let's not forget that again."

"Not for a moment, I promise." Once more they sealed their bargain with a kiss that left him a little weak in the knees. He sat down in Alan's chair and pulled her into his lap.

She came willingly, snuggling close. "You look good in this chair," she said. "Very executive."

"You look good in it, too. We'll have to get another one." He began to nuzzle her throat, just beneath her ear. She shivered a little and wound her arms around his neck.

"We told Kent we'd only be a moment," she said, sounding as breathless as he felt which pleased him no end.

"Mmm." He lowered his head for another kiss but she held him off with a hand against his chest. "I know," he said. "We need to get back downstairs to our guests."

"And to our family."

He covered her hand with his, rubbed his fingers across the warmth of her wedding band, grateful that she was wearing it again, that she was his again. "What do you say, Patsy-girl? Ready to take this new ride together?"

"Yes," she said. "All the way to Victory Lane."

* * * * *

For the Grossos, secrets are woven into the fabric of their lives.
Watch for the latest shocking developments in the Grosso saga in
NASCAR: HIDDEN LEGACIES,
Harlequin's officially licensed NASCAR romance series, in 2009.

Look for
SCANDALS AND SECRETS
by Ken Casper
and
BLACK FLAG, WHITE LIES
by Jean Brashear.
Available in February 2009.

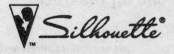

NASCAR

Abby Gaines
CHECKERED PAST

NASCAR team owner Chad Matheson is most comfortable when he's in control. But his control took a time-out when he impulsively wed hotel heiress Brianna Hudson. Two years later, Brianna holds the keys to a much-needed sponsorship for Chad's team, and Chad is determined to keep things between them strictly business. The last thing he needs is anyone finding out that they're still Mr. and Mrs.!

**Available March 2009
wherever books are sold.**

www.GetYourHeartRacing.com

NASCAR18521